one dog AND HIS boy

EVA IBBOTSON

Scholastic Inc.

To Milly, Hugo, and Hilding,
three very important dogs

This book was originally published in hardcover by Scholastic Press in 2012.

ISBN 978-0-545-48441-1

12 11 10 9 8 7 6 5 4 3   15 16 17 18 19/0

Printed in the U.S.A. 40
First Scholastic paperback printing, February 2014

The text was set in ITC Legacy Serif Book.
Book design by Whitney Lyle

ACKNOWLEDGMENT

I owe a great debt of gratitude to Toby Ibbotson
for the help and encouragement he gave me
in the writing of this book.

CONTENTS

1

Hal's Birthday

All Hal had ever wanted was a dog.

He had wanted one for his last birthday and for the birthday before, and for Christmas, and now that his birthday was coming around again he wanted one more desperately than ever. He had read about dogs and dreamed about dogs; he knew how to feed them and how to train them. But whenever he asked his mother for a dog she told him not to be silly.

"How could we have a dog? Think of the mess — hairs on the carpet and scratch marks on the door, and the smell.... Not to mention puddles on the floor," said Albina Fenton, and shuddered.

And when Hal said that he would see to it that it didn't smell and would take it out again and again so that it didn't make puddles, she looked hurt.

"You have such a beautiful home," she told her son, "I would have thought you would be grateful."

This was true in a way. Hal's parents were rich; they lived in a large modern house in the suburbs with carpets so thick that your feet sank right into them and silk curtains that swept to the floor. There were three new cars in the garage — one for Albina, one for her husband, and one for the maid to use when she took Hal to school — and five bathrooms with gold taps and power showers, and a sauna. In the kitchen every kind of gadget hummed and buzzed — squeezers and coffeemakers and extractors — and the patio was tiled with marble brought in specially from Italy.

But in the whole of the house there was nothing that was alive. Not the smallest beetle, not the frailest spider, not the shyest mouse — Albina Fenton and the maids who came and went saw to that. And in the garden there were no flowers — only raked gravel — because flowers mean earth and mess.

• • •

Although he knew it was silly to go on hoping, Hal decided he would have a last try. Three days before his tenth birthday he got up early and padded across the deep blue carpet, which was going to be replaced in the coming week because blue, his mother said, was out of fashion. He had said he liked blue, but his mother had just smiled at him in that rather regretful way that meant that he had said something foolish.

Now he turned off his night-light shaped like a flying saucer and wondered why he seemed to sleep just as badly with the flying saucer night-light as he had done with the night-light in the shape of a skyscraper.

Then he went into his bathroom and washed carefully, making sure that he didn't miss anything, and cleaned his teeth extra hard with his electric toothbrush before spraying his mouth with the high-pressure breath freshener fixed to the wall.

He wanted to have everything right before he wrote the note to his mother because it was important. If she took notice of it, everything would turn out all right, but if she didn't . . .

So now he sat down at his specially designed writing desk and found a pen and a piece of headed notepaper, because his parents hated anything to be scrappy, and wrote very, very carefully:

PLEASE CAN I HAVE A DOG FOR MY BIRTHDAY? PLEASE?

He wrote it out three times because he wanted the writing to be really good — his parents had moved him from his last school because they said he wasn't making enough progress — and then he padded across the corridor and pushed the note through his mother's bedroom door. There was no point in writing a note to his father because his father was in Dubai, or perhaps Hong Kong. Or even Tokyo. Hal could never be certain, though he tried very hard to keep track of his father's business travels. His father was a "frequent flyer" and more often in the air than on the ground.

Albina Fenton, Hal's mother, was in her walk-in wardrobe, trying to decide what to wear.

"Really, everything's in rags," she muttered, passing along a row of glittering evening dresses, then back along a line of tailored suits, opening drawers of frilly blouses and embroidered scarves. "I'll have to throw most of it away and start again. Some serious shopping is required."

When she came out of the wardrobe, she saw that someone had pushed a note under her door and her heart sank. It would be Hal. She hadn't forgotten his birthday; on the contrary, she had made all sorts of arrangements. She had ordered a gift pack from Hamleys and another from Harrods. They would pick out presents suitable for his age group and deliver them the day before and they had never failed her yet. A well-known caterer was bringing in the food and she had booked an entertainer for the party — but Hal had been difficult about the party because they had moved him from his old school to another one that was more suitable in every way, with the right kind of children, and for some reason Hal had been slow to make new friends.

She picked up the note. If only he isn't on about the same thing, she thought.

But he was, and now she had to explain to him once again how impossible it was and had to endure it while Hal turned away and bit his lower lip and looked like a penniless orphan instead of a boy who had everything he could want in the world.

"It really isn't fair," she said to her friends when they came for morning coffee and Hal had been taken to his activities club by the maid. "I do everything for that boy and he is never thankful."

Her friends all had names that began with G: Glenda and Geraldine and Gloria — and they were quick to sympathize.

"But he does look a bit peaked," said Glenda. "I tell you what, I've read somewhere that they do kissograms for children on their birthdays. Or huggograms, I suppose they would be. They send someone dressed like a chimpanzee or some other animal, and he sings a funny song and delivers a message. Maybe they could get someone dressed like a dog?"

After her friends had gone, Albina rang her husband's office and asked his secretary to get a message through to him in Dubai. "Remind him that it's Hal's birthday on Thursday," she said. "He'll be able to pick up a present for him in the duty-free."

Really there wasn't any more she could do, thought Albina, and she picked up a furniture catalogue from the pile on the coffee table. Everybody said that beige was the "in" color this year; she'd have to get rid of the white carpet in the dining room. . . . Not that they'd be here much longer: She really felt quite shamed living in a house without a swimming pool.

Right up to the last minute, Hal went on hoping.

He would open his eyes on the morning of his birthday and hear a snuffling noise outside the door and the dog would come running in. . . . Sometimes the dog was brown and fluffy, sometimes it was white with a smooth coat. Hal didn't mind what it looked like; it would be alive, and it would belong to him, and it would be there when his father was in Dubai and his mother was out with her friends and he was alone in the house with the maid who changed every month and was always so homesick and so sad.

But the phantom dog remained a phantom. Nobody scratched on the door when Hal's birthday came and the sound of barking that made Hal's heart beat fast turned out to be in the street. Hal dressed and went downstairs, where his mother waited beside the breakfast table piled high with packages. Hamleys was not the best-known toy shop in London for nothing; they had sent the latest Xbox game and a new board game and a laser gun and a radio-controlled metal-detecting car. Harrods had sent an iPod and a giant chemistry set and a Roboquad. . . .

"Now are you happy?" said his mother, watching him as he opened his presents, and he said yes, he was, and she told him that his father would be back that evening and would bring something from the airport.

"Did my grandparents send me anything?" asked Hal, and Albina sighed and produced a small packet wrapped in brown paper.

Her husband's parents were poor and lived in a small cottage on the Northumbrian coast. They had come on a visit once when Hal was small, carrying their belongings in an ancient suitcase tied up with string — and really it had been impossible not to be ashamed of them. They hadn't come again, but they sent the most peculiar gifts for Hal at Christmas and on his birthday. If one couldn't afford a proper present, surely it was better to do nothing than send a seashell or a piece of rock, thought Albina. Yet Hal always looked pleased with their gifts, and now he gazed at something small and brown and crumbly as he had not looked at any of his other things.

"It's a sea horse," he said, looking at the note that came with it. "It got washed up on one of the rocks. The fishermen say that it brings luck."

So Hal took his presents upstairs and played with them, and in the afternoon the van arrived with the party tea and the birthday cake shaped like a pair of sneakers (because nothing that Albina ordered was shaped like itself, and a cake that looked like a cake would have bored her very much). Then the friends came — only they weren't really his friends; he had left those at his old school — and played with his toys and broke the metal-detecting car and tipped the chemistry set onto the floor.

But after they had had tea and watched a magician there came a surprise.

A van drew up outside; the bell rang — and then the door opened and a . . . thing . . . burst into the room. It was big and dressed in a yellow furry skin, and it had floppy black ears, a lolling pink tongue, and a tail.

For a moment it pranced about on two legs; then it dropped down on all fours and crawled toward Hal and an odd strangled noise came from it that sounded like "Woof, woof."

When it reached Hal, it dropped a big greeting card from its mouth — and in a hoarse voice it began to sing.

"I am your Birthday Doggie,

Your Doggie for the day.

Just pat me and I'll —"

But the song broke off with a splutter because Hal had gone mad.

"Stop it. Come out of there," he yelled, pulling at the creature's head. "How dare you?" He gave a last tug, and the sweaty red face of the man from the Huggograms Agency stared at him. "How dare you pretend to be a dog!" And he began to kick at the man's shins. "You're disgusting. Get out. Go away."

But Alfred Potts, the man inside the suit, had worked hard at his routine. He hadn't had a cigarette for a whole hour, and he'd cut down on the beer before he came, and he wasn't going to be kicked by a flea-sized kid.

"Now you just pipe down, will you," he said, gripping Hal's arm. "Here's your mum trying to give you a bit of fun, you ungrateful little —"

But before he could finish, Hal slipped from his grasp and ran sobbing out of the room.

And that was the end of the party.

It was late in the evening before the big Mercedes came up the drive and disappeared into the underground garage. A few minutes later Donald Fenton came in and was greeted by his wife.

"Have you got something for Hal?" she said hurriedly. "You haven't forgotten it's his birthday?"

Mr. Fenton clapped his hand over his mouth. He had forgotten. "I was in a meeting till an hour before the plane was due to leave. I nearly didn't make it."

"Oh dear! He kept asking if you'd be back. Well, go and say good night to him anyway; he's upset." And she explained about Mr. Potts and the huggogram.

Donald went slowly upstairs. He shouldn't have forgotten Hal's birthday, but he hadn't had a minute to himself all day — and the boy would have had tons of presents — Albina always saw to that. When he was

Hal's age all he'd had for his birthday was a home-made fishing rod.

Hal was sitting up in bed, waiting. He looked small and peaked and there were dark rings under his eyes.

"I've come straight from the airport," explained his father. "I'm afraid I haven't been able to get you a present, but we'll go shopping tomorrow. I can get away early. Is there anything you'd like?"

Hal shook his head. "All I ever wanted was a dog."

But he spoke listlessly; it was all over. That horrible man smelling of cigarettes and beer had somehow destroyed his dream.

Mr. Fenton looked at his son — and then he had an idea. "All right, Hal. We'll go out tomorrow and get one."

Downstairs, Albina Fenton heard a shriek of joy coming from Hal's room. "What is it?" she asked her husband when he came downstairs. "What's going on?"

Donald was smiling, looking very pleased with himself.

"I've told him we'll get a dog. Tomorrow."

"A dog! You're mad, Donald. I've told you and I've told Hal, I absolutely won't have my house destroyed by an animal."

"It's only for the weekend, Albina. They don't rent them out for longer than that."

"Who doesn't? What are you talking about?"

"The Easy Pets people. It's a place where they rent out dogs — it's around the corner from the office. My secretary told me about it. You can get any dog you like for an hour or a day — people rent them when they want to impress their friends or go into the country. They're very carefully chosen — house-trained and all."

"Yes, but what happens when it's time to take the dog back? Are you going to tell Hal it's only for the weekend?"

"Good heavens, no! By the time the dog has to go back, Hal will be tired of him — you know how quickly children get bored with the things you give them. He only played with that indoor space projector we got him for Christmas for a couple of days and it cost the earth."

"Well, I hope you're right. I really couldn't stand any fuss."

"I am right," said Donald firmly.

And anyway, when it was time for the dog to go back he'd be on the way to New York.

2

Easy Pets

The Easy Pets Dog Agency was owned by a couple called Myron and Mavis Carker. The Carkers were greedy and selfish and they liked making money more than anything in the world.

But they were clever. They had realized that nowadays most people didn't want anything to last for a long time. People changed their houses and their cars again and again; they changed their children's schools and the places where they went for holidays — they even changed their wives or their husbands when they looked like they were becoming a bit ordinary and dull.

So why would they want to hang on to their dogs? The slogan "A Dog Is for Life and Not Just for Christmas" simply wasn't true for a great many people. Dogs, like children, were a tie; you couldn't do exactly what you wanted with a dog in the household.

On the other hand, dogs were nice. They were fun, and some were very beautiful. To be seen with a graceful, freshly groomed borzoi in the park, or a frolicsome fox terrier, was very agreeable. So what could be more sensible than just to rent a dog — for an hour, or an afternoon, or even a weekend? All the dogs would be purebred animals with long pedigrees, and they could even be color matched with the clothes of the person who was hiring them: a red setter to go with an autumn outfit of russet and crimson, or a snowy Pyrenean mountain dog for a man or woman who liked to wear white.

Of course renting such a dog would be very expensive; the dogs wouldn't just have to be groomed and dewormed and examined regularly by a vet; they would have to have their hair done, tied up in a tuft like a shih tzu's, or shaved in parts like a poodle — and that meant regular visits from hairdressers and beauticians. But people would pay, the Carkers had been sure of that, and they were right. A year after Easy Pets opened, the Carkers were on the way to becoming really rich. And because they had to pay out to so many specialists to help them, they made sure that the kennel maid who did the ordinary work of cleaning and feeding the dogs did not have to be paid much. She was a young girl called Kayley, who came in each morning on the train from Tottenham, and worked all hours of the day because she loved dogs — and as you would expect, the dogs loved her.

The Easy Pets building was on a fashionable street in the middle of London next to a row of expensive shops, but at the back there was a big compound where the dogs slept and a yard where they took their exercise. Kayley woke them early and reassured the dogs that had had bad dreams, like the huge English mastiff who, quite by mistake, had bitten off her mistress's little finger when she was being fed a sausage, and had never been punished. Not being punished when you feel you ought to have been is very upsetting for dogs, and the mastiff still suffered in the night. Then Kayley took the dogs out for a short run in the yard and gave them their breakfast.

After that, they went to be washed and groomed and have their hair done and their nails polished and their teeth cleaned — and those of the dogs that wore their hair tied up away from their faces were given fresh ribbons, and those like the Afghan who needed extra brushing were taken away to a special dressing room. Then the dogs were sprayed, each with a special scent mixed by a lady who kept a perfume shop, because the smell of dog wasn't thought to be right for the rich people who took the animals out. The Saint Bernards' scent was called Mountain Glory, the poodles were sprayed with something called Dancer, and the collies were covered in Heather Mist. The dogs disliked these scents more than anything — a dog's smell is as much a part of him as his bark or the way he holds his tail — and they did their best to lick themselves and one another and roll on the ground, but it was almost impossible to get the beastly stuff off.

Then when they were ready for the day's work, they were taken to the front of the building, where there were a number of rooms with elegant cages and soft lighting and fitted carpets. Over each cage was the dog's name and above that the name of the breeder he came from. The dogs were not allowed toys — rubber balls or squeaky animals or plastic bones — to chew on because their cages had to be kept tidy to impress the people who came to pick out the dog they wanted. They just had to sit still and look desirable.

When they had first come to Easy Pets the dogs were full of hope. They had thought every time someone came for them it was someone who wanted a companion for life. Someone who was going to give them a home and to whom they would belong. They had gone off with their heads held high and their tails signaling their happiness — but always and always they were brought back, whether it was after an hour or a day . . . back to their cages and to the waiting.

They had one another, and they had Kayley, and they made the best of it, but it was hard.

In Room A there were five dogs. It was the smallest of the rooms and it was rather special because it was next to the little cubbyhole of an office where Kayley worked when she was not out in the yard, and the dogs who spent the day there had become firm friends.

The largest was Otto, a Saint Bernard with a tan-and-white face, and deep-set mournful eyes. Otto was wise and strong but gentle. He had had a tragedy in his life: His mother, who was an exceptionally large and heavy dog even for a Saint Bernard, had rolled over onto her puppies by mistake and squashed them, and only Otto had survived. This was in the mountains of Switzerland in a famous monastery where Saint Bernards had been bred for centuries to find people trapped in the snow and bring them to safety.

When something like that has happened to you, you don't waste time fussing about small things. Otto had grown into a brave and useful rescue dog, but when a rich young man had insisted on buying him and taking him to England, Otto had made the best of it, though he had been so happy with the monks. Even when the silly young man found that he could not keep a Saint Bernard in a London flat and sold him to Mr. Carker, Otto somehow managed to stay dignified and calm, and to soothe the other dogs when they complained about the food or the disgusting perfume or the boredom.

Next to Otto was a dog as small as Otto was big — a tiny Pekinese called Li-Chee with golden hair down to the ground and a black scrunched-up face. Li-Chee adored Otto; when they were loose in the compound at night, he curled up as close to Otto as he could, and when the Saint Bernard woke he sometimes felt that he had five legs — four of his own and one that was really a Pekinese. Pekes are lion dogs bred to be the companions of Chinese emperors, and the guardians of palaces and temples — and Li-Chee was as fierce and cross as Otto was silent and calm.

The cage beside the Peke was occupied by a black standard poodle. Francine's coat was clipped and trimmed in the fussy way that people expect of poodles, with fluffy pom-poms on her legs and tail and a close-shaven backside, and she was usually rented out by actresses and show people who wanted something glamorous. But inside, Francine was a practical, hardworking dog and exceedingly clever. Her family had been circus performers for generations, doing incredibly difficult acts: running up ladders, jumping through rings of fire, balancing balls on their noses. . . . Francine had loved the life of the circus — the companionship, the traveling in a caravan between one site and the next. But then someone had said training animals to perform was cruel and the circus had been shut down and now she had to sit still all day in a cage waiting to be chosen.

Across from Otto, Li-Chee, and Francine was a rough-haired collie called Honey. Honey was very beautiful, with her long coat of black and white and sable and her soft and trusting eyes. But she was not easy to rent out because she couldn't stop herding things, and because there were no sheep in London she herded anything she could find. She had herded a whole nursery school of little children onto the bandstand in the park, and kept a dozen squawking ducks penned up in a bus shelter.

Honey had been a highly trained sheepdog before she came, but the farmer who owned her had gone bankrupt and had to sell her. All the dogs missed being useful; but for a collie, not being able to work is agony. The others worried about her. Mr. Carker always sounded angry when she was returned early — and they knew what happened to dogs who had displeased Mr. Carker — they simply disappeared and were not seen again.

The last inmate of Room A was an unpleasant female who lay on a special satin cushion with a hot water bottle under her stomach. Queen Tilly was a Mexican hairless, a small twitchy dog with naked spotted skin and legs like sticks. They are a rare breed and most of them are nice, though delicate and shivery, but Tilly had belonged to a wealthy heiress before she came to Easy Pets, and had eaten off silver plates and slept on her owner's silken pillows, and she behaved as though nothing was good enough for her. The other dogs had tried to be friendly when she first came, but she just tossed her head and yawned. The only time she spoke was when her hot water bottle cooled down and then she yapped and squealed till Kayley came and heated it up for her. She was the most expensive of all the dogs for hire and actually she wasn't worth the money.

There was one extra cage in Room A, which at present was empty.

• • •

It had stopped raining and Otto, whose cage faced the window, saw people shutting up their umbrellas, which meant that a borrower would come soon. He sat up very straight in his cage and the other dogs followed his example.

At ten o'clock Kayley brought in a lady dressed in a very elegant black skirt with a purple blouse, and heels so high that she could only totter.

"I think Francine will suit you," Kayley said, going over to the poodle's cage. "She's an extremely intelligent dog and used to restaurants."

"She'll certainly go with my outfit," said the lady. "You see, it's a bit tricky — I met this man at a party last night and he said he adored dogs so I said I adored dogs, too, and he asked me out to lunch. So I thought I would take a dog along and pretend it was mine — don't you think it's a good idea?"

Kayley didn't. She thought it was a perfectly ridiculous idea, but she was used to the batty ideas of the hirers, so she just smiled and went on stroking Francine's head through the bars of the cage.

"I suppose I could have something smaller, but

then it would have to sit on my lap and it might leave hairs on my skirt. Or it would get stepped on by the waiters."

"I think you will find Francine just right," said Kayley again. "She's used to lying under tables. The only thing is, she's very musical — if it's the kind of place with an orchestra playing, she might start to join in. Especially if they were to play a waltz."

But the lady said no, it wasn't that kind of place, it was a very expensive, quiet restaurant, the kind where people talked in low voices, usually about the food.

So Francine was taken away to be fitted with a rhinestone collar and have her ribbon changed for one that would match the blouse of the lady who was going to pretend that Francine was her own dog, and they went away.

When the poodle had been gone for an hour, a thin, worried-looking woman came and said she wanted a very large dog to protect her for the afternoon, because she was going to visit her son, who lived in a district where there were a lot of foreigners and people who were very poor, and she was afraid of being attacked.

Kayley wanted to say that people who were poor or foreign did not attack old ladies any more than anybody else — she knew this because the people she lived among were poor, and many of them came from other countries — but she wanted Otto to have an outing so she said nothing and went to fetch Otto's collar and leash.

Some dogs from the other rooms were borrowed, but not Honey or Li-Chee, who spent a boring afternoon dozing in their cages, while Queen Tilly went off to the infirmary to have her body massaged with olive oil because her skin was flaking.

On the following day an elderly woman came for the Pekinese because she had to go and see a friend who was even older, but the visit was not a success.

There is absolutely nothing wrong with old ladies, but when your ancestors have been bred to ride on the saddle of the emperor when he gallops off to war, you do not feel like being told that you are an itsy-bitsy little doggie, aren't you — and though no dog from Easy Pets ever bit people, Li-Chee growled and showed his teeth and was brought back early.

Honey was hired by a man who had seen all the

Lassie films when he was a boy and wanted to be photographed with her on the towpath near his house, and Francine was borrowed again by the woman who had told the man she had met at a party that the poodle was hers.

But on the day after that, something unexpected happened.

Kayley arrived early and came to the compound with her buckets of food and said good morning to the dogs as she always did. But this morning she was not alone. Trotting beside her, a piece of string around its makeshift collar, was a dog.

It was not a make of dog that any of the others recognized. It was white with a brown splodge over one ear and another brown splodge above its tail, and smallish like a fox terrier, and it had bat ears like a corgi, whereas its violently wagging tail was a bit like the flagpole tail of a beagle. But it was not any of those things. It was something that had never before been seen in Easy Pets — a mongrel.

Kayley let the mongrel off the leash and he hurled himself joyfully at the nearest dog, which fortunately was Otto. As far as he could see he had been given a present of thirty or so new friends and he didn't know whether to bark ecstatically, roll over, or lie on his back and wave his legs in the air, so he tried to do all these things at the same time.

Kayley took Otto and Francine aside.

"I want you to be very nice to him," she said. Kayley always spoke to the dogs as though they were people and of course they understood her perfectly. "He's a stray. I found him last night outside my house and no one seems to want him."

Kayley lived in a small house in Tottenham with her family. They were very poor and their landlord was a horrible man who wouldn't allow them to keep pets and didn't do their repairs either. The night before, she had gone out to the take-out place for supper with her family and found this small white creature, wet through and shivering on their doorstep.

The dogs clustered around, sniffing the newcomer. He smelled of dog and not the nasty scents they had sprayed on them, and though he was a bit enthusiastic and puppyish they were happy to welcome him. Only Li-Chee growled a little because Otto was being very nice to the new arrival and he was jealous.

"I've got a plan," Kayley told the dogs. "I don't know if it'll work, but in the meantime, if you could just play with him and make it seem as though he belongs."

She let them out into the yard and ran around with them while they had their exercise, and with such a crowd of dogs the little stray did not stand out.

When it was time for the dogs to go to their cages, Kayley slipped the mongrel into the empty cage in Room A. There was nothing to do now except wait for Mr. Carker to come on his daily inspection, and hope for the best.

He came as soon as the dogs were settled, wearing the white smock he wore to impress the clients, and carrying a clipboard, on which were his notes. For Mr. Carker kept notes on everything: how often a particular dog had been borrowed, whether the client had been pleased with him, and the exact profit the firm had made. Dogs to Mr. Carker were just machines for making money and any animal that did not look like it was earning its keep was sent away at once.

"Well, how are we doing this morning?" asked Mr.

Carker, and Kayley said that everything was fine, and that the headmistress of a primary school had rung up and wanted to rent Otto for a whole day as an end-of-term treat for the children.

Then he stopped at the cage with the little white stray that Kayley had brought in.

His face darkened. "What on earth is going on here? Are you mad, girl? This is a mongrel. Who brought him in and what is he doing here?"

"Please, sir, I brought him in, but he's not a mongrel." Kayley was a truthful girl, but if a life could be saved by telling lies, then one just had to go ahead. "He's a new breed. They're just going to register him at the Kennel Club. I got him for my birthday, but our landlord won't let us keep dogs."

Mr. Carker scowled at the newcomer, who was wagging his tail and giving little barks of greeting.

"It's true," said Kayley. "Honestly. He's a . . . Tottenham terrier. They're becoming quite fashionable. I saw one at a dog show in Brighton."

Mr. Carker hesitated. Kayley was very knowledgeable about dogs, and it wouldn't do to be ignorant of a new breed, but he was suspicious.

"I've got his pedigree at home," said Kayley. "Couldn't we try him? Maybe we could charge a bit less as he's new."

"Well, perhaps." A Tottenham terrier. It had a good ring to it. "But mind you, if he hasn't been hired by the end of the week, then he goes. If you can't take him, there's always the cat and dog shelter. I won't have an animal here that doesn't earn its keep." And as Kayley bent down and stroked the dog through the bars: "Did you hear me?"

"Yes, sir."

At the door Mr. Carker turned. "You'd better find a name for him and get it put on his cage."

"Yes, sir," said Kayley again.

But she already had a name. She had found it when she looked into the mongrel's eyes. They were dark and trusting and full of intelligence — but they were not completely equal. On one eye was a splodge, a single fleck of gold.

"He's called Fleck," she said.

But Mr. Carker had already gone.

3

The Tottenham Terrier

Left alone in Room A, the dogs looked at their new roommate. They were kind and caring dogs and they were worried.

The Tottenham terrier, or whatever he was, was altogether too hopeful and too excitable for life as a rental dog with Easy Pets.

"Calm down," Otto wanted to say. "Take it easy. Just sit in the front of the cage; don't throw yourself at people."

But Fleck could no more calm down than he could fly. He was here with new friends, at the beginning of a great adventure. He wasn't quite certain what the great adventure was, but it would be to do with someone who would come for him, and who would love him and whom he would love. The little mongrel didn't understand that Mr. Carker would send him away if he had not been borrowed by five o'clock on Friday and if he had, he would not have worried because he was absolutely certain that somebody would come.

A mongrel and a crossbreed are not the same thing. A crossbreed is a mixture of two breeds only, and is considered quite respectable — like a labradoodle — but a mongrel can have six or more different strains of dog in him. And in Fleck's case the six strains, whatever they were, all seemed to be breeds that were used to serving people and looking after them and belonging.

At ten o'clock, Otto stopped trying to calm Fleck and all the others dogs fell silent because that was when, outside the window, a guide dog called Grace came past, taking her blind mistress to the shops. Grace was a golden retriever, and while all the others admired Grace for her skill and her hard work, Otto did more than that. Otto really worshipped Grace.

Soon after that Mr. Carker brought in a man in a

chauffeur's cap and Queen Tilly was taken away to have her special jacket put on — one with snaps down the back so that people could open it to see that she really was hairless all over — and then the chauffeur carried her to a waiting Rolls-Royce, where a lady who was going to show her off at a fancy coffee gathering in her mansion was waiting.

Renting out Queen Tilly always put Mr. Carker in a good humor because he got so much money for her, and when he passed Fleck's cage he laughed.

"No one's come for the Tottenham terrier, I see," he said to Kayley. "And no one will, if you ask me — I've never seen such an ugly little brute."

He was one of those people who think that dogs can't understand anything that humans say and Kayley had to stay behind and pet Fleck before he was his old self.

It was a long day for the small white dog. Otto was taken away in the middle of the morning by the headmistress of the school whose children had asked for a dog for the day as their end-of-term treat, and Honey was borrowed by a man who was meeting a rich friend at a country club and wanted to look sporting. Then

Francine went off with the lady who was still hood-winking her new boyfriend, making him believe that the poodle was hers.

Early in the afternoon a couple came who had been told to lose weight and go for walks and they thought taking exercise might be less boring if they did it with a dog.

"This is a nice dog," said Kayley, showing them Fleck. "He's got a lovely nature."

But the man said he was an odd-looking creature and if they had to go to the park, they might as well take something with a bit of class, and they went through into Room B and picked out a saluki with long silky ears and an arched back.

Then Li-Chee was taken away to have his ears syringed and only Fleck was left. He tried hard to amuse himself but it was very lonely without the other dogs, and though his cage was comfortable it was still a cage, and without meaning to, he began to howl softly.

In a second, Kayley was in the room.

"Oh hush, Fleck. Please be quiet. Mr. Carker really hates dogs to howl."

She fondled his head, and he stopped at once — but there was no hope now that anyone would come for Fleck that day; the hiring stopped at five. And that meant there were only two more days for the Tottenham terrier to earn his keep and become an Easy Pet.

It was always late when Kayley got home. Mr. Carker did not live in the Easy Pets building — he and Mrs. Carker had a very elegant apartment a few streets away — and it was Kayley's job to make sure that the dogs were safely in their compound, and the building was locked and the burglar alarm put on at the end of the day. And even when all that was done, she had an hour's journey on the train.

But she did not come home to an empty house — far from it. Kayley lived with her mother, her grandfather, her twin brothers, who were still at school, and her ten-year-old sister, Pippa.

The O'Brians were poor. Kayley's father had been killed in an accident on a building site, and though her mother had a job sewing for a wealthy lady called Mrs. Naryan, and her grandfather had his pension, money was very short. The little house was shabby, the carpets were threadbare, greasy smells from the burger chain next door wafted through the window, but when Kayley came home she was hugged and petted, and when her family asked how her day was, they really wanted to know because they thought that her job as kennel maid to the Carkers was the most interesting you could imagine.

And the person who hugged the hardest and wanted to know the most was ten-year-old Pippa.

"Did your plan work?" she asked now. "Has Mr. Carker let him stay?"

Fleck had spent the night at the O'Brians' and all of them wanted to know about the stray.

"He's given him till Friday night. If nobody borrows him by then, he's going to send him away."

Pippa was a sturdy, cheerful girl — but now her face puckered up.

"To the cat and dog shelter?"

Kayley nodded.

"Well, I think it's wicked. He knows perfectly well they can only keep the dogs for three weeks and then if no one's given them a home, they have to have them put down. It's just a sneaky way of getting other people to do your dirty work."

Pippa knew all about the dogs that Kayley looked after. On Sundays she went along to help Kayley with the cleaning and the feeding, and she was determined, when she was old enough, to follow in her sister's footsteps.

"He's got to let Fleck stay," she said now.

"If only he'd see . . ." said Kayley. "Mind you, Fleck shouldn't really be a rental dog — he's a bit loopy, the way he goes on about people. He's like Snow White when she sings that song. You know: 'Someday My Prince Will Come.' He's convinced his prince will come — or his princess. You should see his eyes every time someone comes into the room." She shrugged. "Anyway, we've got to make up a pedigree for him before the morning. Mr. Carker wants one to put over his cage."

Supper was ready then, and the twins needed help with their homework, and after that Grandfather had to be wheeled down to the corner store to buy his lottery ticket.

But at last everything was cleared away and Kayley

and Pippa went into the little bedroom they shared and started to work on Fleck's pedigree.

"Pedigrees are always complicated and a bit ridiculous," said Kayley. "The dogs are called things like Wilhelmina Bossyboots of Kilimanjaro. And the more highly bred the dogs are, the longer the names."

They spent a long time thinking, but in the end they decided that Fleck's mother had been called Rodelinda of Mersey Drive because that was the name of the street where they had been for takeout on the night they found Fleck.

"And his father could be Frederick the Fifth of Fillongley," said Pippa. "It might bring him luck if he was called after the farm."

Fillongley was the name of the farm that had belonged to the O'Brians till their great-great-grandfather went bankrupt. There was a painting of it above the mantelpiece, and whatever else occasionally got pawned or sold, the picture of Fillongley Farmhouse stayed where it was.

They went on making up pedigrees, getting wilder and sillier till it was time for Pippa to go to bed.

When she came to tuck her sister in for the night, Kayley said, "You'd better pray for Fleck. Pray that there's someone out there who wants him."

"Yes, I will," said Pippa.

And she did. But Pippa wasn't a gentle and accepting girl like Kayley. Pippa was a fighter. She wanted to go out into the world and do battle for the rights of stray dogs everywhere to have a decent home. And not just stray dogs. Everyone who was poor and treated unfairly by life. When she was six, she had dragged a girl called Myrtle to the school toilet and flushed her head down the bowl because Myrtle had been bullying a small child in the kindergarten class.

When later Kayley slipped into the bed beside her sleeping sister, she could hear, quite distinctly, the sound of Pippa grinding her teeth.

Back in the compound at night, Fleck cheered up again. Though he was careful not to take up Li-Chee's place by Otto's left foot, he slept with his roommates. Otto was tired — there is nothing more exhausting than being petted by twenty-five small children — but he had time to give Fleck a good-night lick before everybody slept.

But the next morning, and the morning after, which was the fateful Friday, the waiting began again. Fleck now had his name above his cage, and his pedigree, which Kayley had inscribed on a serious-looking piece of paper, and he had a number — Number 51. If only someone came and rented him out, just one person, just for a short time, everything would be all right.

But the day crawled on, and again nobody came for the little dog. The other dogs became more and more concerned; they understood full well what happened to dogs that never left their cages. They were taken away by two men in brown coats and bundled into a traveling crate and never seen again, and they could hardly bear to watch as Fleck pressed himself against the wire and looked up with his unequal eyes as the borrowers came — but not for him. He knew better now than to howl, and Kayley came whenever she could to stroke him — but as the minutes ticked away, the atmosphere in Room A became more and more tense, and when Queen Tilly started one of her squealing sessions because her hot water bottle had cooled down, the others forgot themselves and started to growl.

Then at three o'clock Mr. Carker came in with his clipboard.

"It seems there isn't much call for Tottenham terriers," he told the little dog. "We'll have to get rid of you. Can't have you eating me out of house and home."

And he told Kayley to expect the men from the Canine Transport Company, who were coming to take the dog away.

He went out and shut the door and Fleck was left cowering in the corner of his cage. He recognized Mr. Carker's tone all too well. He had heard it often in his hard life as a stray.

Then at four-thirty, a large Mercedes drew up in the street outside, and a man got out, holding the hand of a small boy.

Hal Chooses

Mr. Carker always saw important clients in his office before he took them around, and Mr. Fenton, who was head of International Power Inc., was clearly important.

"I believe you know our terms," he said. "They're laid out in the brochure. Twenty-five pounds an hour, and a deposit of three hundred pounds, returnable when the dog is brought back to us in good condition. Now, for a weekend borrowing we have a special rate —"

"Yes, yes," said Mr. Fenton hurriedly. Hal had been looking out of the window and hadn't been listening. He lowered his voice. "Perhaps you have someone who could show my son around while we deal with the business." He gave Mr. Carker a meaningful look and Mr. Carker caught on quickly. He was very used to people who lied to their children, and he went out into the corridor and shouted for Kayley.

"Will you take the young gentleman through the rooms and show him the dogs?" he said when she came. "He's going to pick one out."

Kayley smiled at Hal and he smiled back. He thought being a kennel maid must be the most wonderful job in the world; and she was so pretty with her wavy dark hair and her deep blue eyes. . . .

"I'm allowed to pick out whichever one I want," Hal told her. "I hope it'll be a young one because dogs can live for fifteen years, can't they, or more, so I'll have him till I'm grown up."

Kayley drew in her breath. She knew that Easy Pets were never rented out for more than three days. So they were tricking the child; she'd seen it done before. "Have you got any special breed in mind?"

Hal shook his head. "No. I just want to look — when I see the right one, I'll know." He looked up at her trustingly. "I'll know at *once*, I'm absolutely sure."

"Yes," said Kayley. "It's often like that. One just knows."

She took him first to Room E, at the back of the building, and stopped by a basset hound, wheezing mightily in the corner of his cage. He was a most attractive dog, and Hal scratched him through the bars of the cage, but he did not say anything. The dog next to him was the mastiff who had bad dreams, and Hal listened openmouthed while Kayley told him the sad story of the swallowed finger.

"She's over it now, but the other dogs are very gentle with her; it's as though they know."

Nobody could help loving the mastiff, but Hal was a sensible boy. It was nearly half-term now, but later he would be at school part of each day; such an enormous dog would not get enough exercise. Next to the mastiff was a beautiful Cavalier King Charles spaniel who obediently lay down on his back with his paws in the air, ready to be scratched or stroked — or even kicked, because these spaniels are such good-natured dogs that they will do anything to give their owners pleasure.

"He's had a bad time, too," said Kayley. "The couple

he belonged to split up and they sent him backward and forward on the train between Edinburgh and London, from one to the other. If he sees a train now, he just sits down and howls."

"Oh, I wish I could have him," said Hal. "He's a marvelous dog," and Kayley nodded, for the spaniel would have been a perfect choice.

But Hal went on to the next cage, past a corgi, past a schnauzer . . . and then through into Room D.

The first dog they came to there was a dalmatian, and Kayley half waited for Hal to say, "That's the one," because since the famous film about dalmatians every child in the world seemed to want one. But again, though Hal scratched him through the bars, and sighed a little — he did not stop. They passed a Lhasa apso, so hairy that it was hard to tell which end was which, and a pug. The dogs were tired now, it was the end of a working day, but when they saw Kayley come with a visitor, they did their best to sit up and greet them politely. A chow . . . a beautiful Tibetan lion dog . . . a Labrador . . .

Hal was looking a little strained now. He had been absolutely certain that he would know when he came to the dog that was for him — yet they had passed so many marvelous dogs and no voice had spoken inside his head and said, "Stop! This is the one."

Suppose he had been mistaken? Suppose there wasn't one dog waiting for him that he would instantly recognize? And Kayley, seeing his anxiety, put her arm around his shoulders and they moved on into the next room, Room C, where she pointed out the special things about each of the dogs they came to: the markings around the eyes of a deerhound, which in the old days had made people think they could tell the future . . . the tight woolly coat of the Irish water spaniel that meant they could swim in the coldest water.

And still Hal marveled at the dogs, and still he shook his head, and still they went on.

Hal's father had come to join them now and he tried to give Hal some advice. "That boxer's got a nice smooth coat — he wouldn't make too much of a mess," he said. Or "I daresay your mother wouldn't mind that little dachshund too much?"

But Hal, with his forehead crumpled up, scarcely heard what his father said. With Kayley beside him, he walked from dog to dog — and looked . . . and did not say the words that everybody waited for.

Room A now. They passed Otto, and Hal stopped to give him an extra scratch between the ears. The beauty of his character shone through — this was a very special dog; and he saw how tenderly Kayley smiled at him. Francine, too; Hal could see through the fussy poodle clipping to her hardworking, steady soul. Then the collie . . . Hal had seen every Lassie film ever made — but still he did not stop. Nor did he stop for the Peke, or Queen Tilly lying on her hot water bottle.

But this was the last room. There was one cage in the corner but it was empty. There were no more dogs.

"I was wrong," he said in a small voice. "I thought I would know."

It didn't matter. Every dog in the place was worth having. He would get Kayley to pick one out for him, but his confidence was gone.

It was at this moment that two men in brown overalls came through the door that led from the street into the cubbyhole.

"We've had a message from the shelter," one of them said. "They've got a burst pipe — the floor's awash and they can't take in any more animals tonight, so we've brought him back. Number fifty-one."

"Where is he?" asked Kayley.

"He's still in his crate out at the back. We were just going to load him up when we got the message. Where do you want him?"

"Bring him in here," said Kayley.

"Oh, we can't do that. Mr. Carker's signed him off — he wouldn't want —"

"Bring him in," repeated the kennel maid.

There was a short pause; then the men shrugged and went out again.

Kayley followed them. There was the sound of a crate being pried open, and something small and white appeared in the doorway. For a moment, Fleck stood still and looked about him. Then like a bullet from a gun he shot across the room and hurled himself at Hal. Almost at the same time, Hal dropped to his knees and held out his arms.

"I told you!" he cried. "I told you I'd know. I told you both of us would know!"

Mr. Carker came in at that point and took everything in.

"Ah, you have found the Tottenham terrier," he said with an oily smile. "We were just about to take him to . . . to a dog show . . . but there's been a delay." He turned to Mr. Fenton. "Of course, for a dog like that, we'd have to charge considerably more. The breed is still very rare."

Mr. Fenton was about to complain, but then he looked at Hal. Or rather he looked at the bundle that was Hal and the dog, seeming to merge into a single thing — and he shrugged and followed Mr. Carker to his office.

"He's called Fleck," said Kayley, when the men had gone. "It's because —"

Hal looked up at her. "I know why — it's because he's got a gold fleck in his left eye."

"Yes," said Kayley. "That is exactly why."

5

First Day

Hal woke feeling . . . unusual. He was warm — but that wasn't so odd. What was odd was that he felt happy. Comfortable. Safe. Not as though he had had bad dreams — not as though he had had dreams at all.

On the other hand his bed was hard. It was surprisingly hard. Then he realized it wasn't a bed at all. He was lying on the floor with his duvet over him, and then he remembered. He had promised not to let Fleck sleep on his bed, and he had kept his promise. But he wasn't going to leave his dog alone on his first day in his new home.

And at this moment a cold nose was thrust into his hand — and Fleck exploded into the glory of a new day. Like his owner, Fleck woke to safety and happiness and warmth. He leapt onto Hal's chest, he licked his ear, he jumped off and rolled over so that Hal could rub his stomach.

But Hal was remembering his mother's words the night before.

"If he makes a puddle on the carpet, he's going into the garage and staying there."

There was no time to lose in getting Fleck out of doors.

Getting dressed was not easy because Fleck had good ideas of how to "help" — putting Hal's socks in interesting places and herding his shoes . . . but when Hal was ready Fleck allowed him to slip on his collar and leash and followed him down the stairs like a model dog walking to heel.

Hal let himself out of the front door and down the drive. The yard, which wasn't really a yard but a lot of raked gravel, stretched away to either side but they reached the road before Fleck lifted his leg. Opposite the house was a private garden belonging to the people on the street but there was a notice on the gate saying *No Dogs or Unaccompanied Children.*

But past the end of the road, where the houses were smaller and not so elegant, there was a park, open to everybody. His mother didn't like taking him there; the children who played in it could be rough — but Fleck thought it looked good. He steamed ahead, looking back at Hal every so often, and then they were through the gate.

It was a very ordinary city park, but Fleck behaved as though he was in paradise. He put his head down and sniffed the whole history of the dogs that had been there recently. He tried eating a tuft of grass and sneezed. He found a fascinating pile of raked leaves. And all the time his ears twitched with eagerness, and his face turned back to Hal, making sure that Hal, too, could smell the smells and feel the earth on his paws, and *share.*

Hal let the dog lead him — and because of that found himself face-to-face with a girl of about his own age with masses of fair hair and bright blue eyes.

She was sitting on a bench reading and was the sort of pretty, self-assured girl who usually frightened Hal, but Fleck liked her immediately.

"He's got a lot of breeds in him, I'd say?" she said, stroking his back, but Hal shook his head.

"He's a Tottenham terrier," he said.

"I've never heard of that," she said. "It must be a new breed. He looks really intelligent. Why don't you let him off the leash?"

"I've only just got him. I'm going to take him to dog training classes next week, but I don't know if he'd come back."

"Of course he'd come back. He loves you."

Hal looked at her. Her words made him feel ridiculously happy. He bent down and unclipped the leash. Fleck shook himself, then took off like a racing greyhound — and disappeared behind a clump of trees.

There was a moment of panic as Hal and the blond girl looked at each other. Supposing he disappeared forever? Then with as much speed as he had raced off, the little dog returned, a streak of white on his way home.

"Told you," said the girl.

But Fleck was now ready to play. He led Hal to a large tree, and raced around it, chasing whatever was in his head — imaginary squirrels, rabbits, rats even. Hal followed him going the other way and they met in the middle. The girl with the blond curls came, too, and a long game of chase followed. It was an oak tree; last year's acorns lay on the ground. Fleck tried one, didn't care for it, spat it out.

Behind the tree was a large hole — obviously the other dogs that had helped to make it were the right kind, because Fleck was delighted with it. He dug his share, with yelps of pleasure. The earth was rich and dark and damp — it must have rained in the night.

Two boys who had been kicking a soccer ball came over. Remembering the boys who had destroyed his birthday toys, Hal was apprehensive, but they were friendly — and let Fleck chase their ball a few times before they wandered off.

"I'd best take him back now," Hal told the blond girl. "I haven't had breakfast yet and my parents will be wondering where I am."

She nodded. "See you tomorrow maybe," she said. "I'll walk with you to the gate."

But the path they took led past a pond — and on the pond were half a dozen ducks.

Fleck stood for a moment, taking stock. The hair on his back rose, growls worthy of a *Steppenwolf* came from him, and before Hal realized what was happening, there was a mighty splash and Fleck was swimming strongly toward the ducks.

The birds squawked indignantly, then took off with a flutter of dripping wings. Fleck swam to and fro for a few minutes, pretending he had only gone in for the exercise; then, as Hal called him, he scrambled out through the reeds.

"Run!" said the girl. "Don't let him get near you." And she took off along the path. But Hal had only been a dog owner for a day. He waited, and Fleck came as close to him as possible and then, most mightily, he shook himself.

"That's a plucky little brute you've got there," said an old man leading a Great Dane. "They're good swimmers, these crossbreeds."

Hal was about to explain that he was a Tottenham terrier — but he was almost as wet as the dog and he put Fleck on the leash and set off for home.

As they came up the drive to his house, Hal began to worry. He had promised his mother that he wouldn't let the dog make puddles, but Fleck was practically a walking puddle all by himself. He decided to go in through the back. Olga, the new maid, was surly; she came from Kazakhstan and hardly spoke a word of English and Hal was afraid of her sulks and her tears. But when she saw him with the soaking little dog, she pulled him into the kitchen, and found a towel and rubbed Fleck till he looked freshly washed rather than bedraggled. Then she found some dry clothes for Hal and pushed him forward into the dining room.

"Mother eats already — go quick . . ." she said.

But she was smiling.

"If I didn't know it was going to be over the day after tomorrow, I couldn't stand it," said Albina. "I found a white hair on the carpet — and another on the footstool. And I nearly fell over the creature's drinking bowl. I do so hate mess!"

Albina's friends — the ones with names beginning with G — were having morning coffee with her and they were very sympathetic.

"I had a friend whose husband brought home an Irish wolfhound," said Glenda. "Imagine it — one swish of his tail and a whole table full of precious ornaments were swept to the floor. And all the husband could say was 'The dog is saying hello.' She divorced him, of course — nothing else to do."

Hal came in then, carrying Fleck for safety, to greet Aunt Gloria and Aunt Glenda and Aunt Geraldine.

"I thought you'd like to see him," he said.

Fleck wanted to get down and say hello properly, with sniffing and rolling over and all that kind of thing, but Hal held him firmly. Aunt Glenda was wearing very full purple harem trousers and pumps with a big tassel on each toe and he had already discovered how fond Fleck was of anything attached to shoes.

"He's not completely trained yet, though he does sit for quite a long time when you tell him to," he told the ladies.

He carried the dog around to each of them as though he was offering them a wonderful present.

Geraldine patted him gingerly, Glenda just smiled nervously, and Gloria said, "Does he bite?"

"Well, I hope Donald knows what he's doing," said Glenda, when Hal had carried the dog out again. "It doesn't look as though he's tired of him yet."

"Donald is sure he will be by tomorrow evening. Hal had to get up early to exercise him — it's a lot of work looking after the things. And frankly, whether there's a fuss or not, I really couldn't go on with this. Suppose he scratches the new coffee table?"

And all of them shuddered at a thought as dreadful as that.

That night, lying on the floor again, covered by his duvet, with Fleck curled up beside him, Hal was thinking. Often and often when you wanted something and then got it, it was a disappointment. He had looked forward to going to the Seychelles for a holiday — his parents had said there would be snorkeling and scuba diving . . . but when he got there he developed a horrible rash from some tropical bug and couldn't go into the water at all. And it was the same with skiing — they'd all gone to Davos and then there wasn't any snow and the hotel was full of people having parties and drinking too much and being sick and they'd come home early.

But having a dog was completely different. He'd wanted it and wanted it and when it happened it was even better than he'd thought it would be. He'd imagined some of it — the companionship and the warmth — but he didn't realize a dog would make you laugh so much, nor that he would help you to make so many friends.

It was extraordinary, too, how much a dog made you see. The hollows in the oak tree . . . and the way the acorns sat so neatly in their cups . . . how the earth clagged together, so dark after rain . . . Hal hadn't even noticed that it had rained.

And how much he made you think. Fleck had found an iron grating over a drain when they went out in the afternoon. The drain had interested him so much that he'd lain down on his stomach, just looking and smelling and investigating, and Hal realized that he'd never before thought about what might live down there, in the black and evil-looking water. Perhaps ancient river spirits, driven from their homes . . . or strange animals washed down through bath drains . . . there might be a whole sewage underworld that no one knew about.

He reached up to turn on his night-light, but Fleck was lying across his feet and Hal didn't want to disturb him. Anyway, he didn't need a night-light now that he had a protector and a friend.

Early the next morning, which was Sunday, Hal wrote a postcard to his grandparents in Northumberland. He had never had anything interesting to tell them, but now he did. He knew how pleased they would be for him, how glad that he had a dog. There was a dog, of course, in their cottage by the sea. Then he addressed the card and took it to the mailbox, with Fleck following at his heels.

They went on to the park and though they did not meet the girl with blond hair, they met the man with the Great Dane and the big dog stood patiently while Fleck went around and around him, admiringly sniffing at each leg. Then they ran to the tree and found the hole and the pile of leaves and it was as though the park was already home.

Sunday was Olga's day off, but today she stopped Hal as he came in and showed him a bone that he could have for Fleck. It was the right kind of bone, not splintery, and Fleck thanked her very beautifully. She had stopped being silent and surly, and Hal realized that she had just been lonely and sad, another thing the dog had made him understand. Apparently she had had a lot of animals at home in Kazakhstan and whenever she couldn't think of the name for whatever the animal was in English, she made the right noise — mooing and bleating and barking and hissing, till both she and Hal were doubled up with laughter.

"What on earth is going on here?" said Albina, coming in just as Olga was pretending to be a goat trying to swallow a bicycle tire. Then she caught sight of Fleck, chewing his bone. "Oh, Hal, he'll make a mess on the floor. Don't bring him into the drawing room, whatever you do."

In the afternoon Hal's parents had been invited to have tea with Sir Richard and Lady Dorothy Graham, who lived in a beautiful house in Richmond near the river, and had three children roughly Hal's age. They were perfectly behaved children, the kind who made Hal want to be sick.

"Only there's no question of taking the dog," said Albina. "Lady Dorothy's house is absolutely spotless — and anyway he'd make marks on the leather of the car."

Albina's Mercedes was upholstered in snow-white Moroccan leather and was the apple of Albina's eye.

"I'm not going without Fleck. Absolutely not," said Hal.

"Well, you can't stay here alone," said Albina.

But to everyone's surprise, Olga, who always had Sunday afternoon off, said she would take Hal to the shopping mall so that he could buy a ball and some toys for Fleck.

So Hal stayed, and had a lovely afternoon. He had not spent any of the birthday money from his Australian godmother and he and Fleck studied squeaky rubber ducks and balls of various sizes and plastic bones and clockwork mice. There were other people there choosing Sunday treats for their pets, and the girl with fair hair Hal had met in the park was buying hamster food.

"We have tea!" said Olga, to Hal's surprise, taking the girl by the arm. "You go ask mother — I have much cake."

So the girl, whose name was Hilary, came to tea and they played with Fleck and threw the squeaky toys for him and he rushed all over the house retrieving them. But when Hilary had gone, and he settled down for a nap in Hal's room, Fleck was not lying on the rubber duck that had been his favorite, but on Hal's blue facecloth, which had slipped from the side of the washbasin onto the floor. And later, when Hal tried to take it from him, he produced his first attempt at a growl and fastened his teeth more firmly around his treasure.

This facecloth, Fleck was saying, is now *mine*.

6

The Trick

Hal was in bed, his father was in his study — but Albina was on her hands and knees on the stairs, searching for dog hairs. Hal had promised he would clean up after the dog wherever he went, but now she could see a hair on the half landing, and something — possibly a speck of mud — on the bottom stair.

She gave a squeak of irritation and reached for the dustpan and brush she had brought. Olga could do it properly, but not until the morning, for the wretched maid always went to bed so early.

Thank goodness this was the last day of having a messy animal around the house. Tomorrow Fleck was going back to where he came from. She really couldn't have stood any more dirt and annoyance.

Going back into the house, Albina stored her dustpan and went to say good night to Hal. He was usually very quiet before she came in — but tonight there was the sound of running footsteps and shouting. He was playing a game with the dog — and then came a crash as something fell to the floor.

She opened the door.

"Oh, Hal, not the night-light! You know how expensive that was. It's a special design and the pieces are handmade to go with the carpet."

She picked up the lamp. It was definitely ruined, the pieces bent. "I don't know how I shall ever replace it."

But Hal didn't seem to be sorry.

"You won't have to," he said cheerfully. "I don't need a night-light anymore. I don't care how dark it is now that I've got Fleck."

Going downstairs again, Albina went in search of her husband.

"I thought you said Hal would be bored with a dog after two days. You promised me."

Donald was in his study. A small earpiece that connected him with the head office in New York hung out of one ear. He hadn't heard a word she said.

Albina repeated her words. "Will you listen? I'm telling you, he isn't sick of the dog and you promised me he would be."

Donald switched off reluctantly.

"Well, whether he's sick of the dog or not, the animal goes back first thing. Make sure you get him there by ten o'clock, otherwise I have to pay for another day's rental. And see that you get all the deposit back. The chap who runs the place is the worst sort of shark."

Albina stared at him. "I'm not taking him back. You're taking him back."

"No, I'm not. I told you, I'm catching the six o'clock plane from Heathrow in the morning. I'm going to New York. I'll be halfway across the Atlantic before the Easy Pets place opens."

"Well, I think that's a bit much. What am I going to tell Hal?"

"Tell him anything you like — but not till the dog's safely back."

Albina was very angry. "It's all very well for you —

having ideas and then flying off and leaving me to pick up the pieces. You do it all the time and I'm tired of it."

"If you think I like flying all over the world, you're mistaken. It's very exhausting. I do it so that you can have a beautiful home and all the clothes you need. If you weren't so extravagant . . ."

They began to quarrel. They were so used to quarreling that they almost forgot what the quarrel was about. This one went on till it was time to go to bed — but by that time Albina had decided that she would get the maid, Olga, to take Hal to the dentist on the following morning — and while he was gone she would bundle the dog up and take him to Easy Pets. By the time Hal got back everything would be over. He would be upset, she could see that, so perhaps it might be an idea to take him shopping in the afternoon. Perhaps a new car racing set . . . or one of those miniature radios shaped like a piece of fruit. She had seen them in the Hamleys catalogue and they looked really cute.

The appointment with the dentist was at ten o'clock.

"Olga will take you," said Hal's mother on the following morning.

"Can I take Fleck? The receptionist is very nice; she'll let me put him in the garden at the back."

"No, Hal, definitely not. No animals are allowed in the office, you know that."

"But —"

"That's enough, Hal. Go and clean your teeth and get ready. You can give Fleck a bone to eat while you're away."

Hal shook his head. "We've only got the kind left that splinters, but I'll stop off on the way back and get a good one. Marrow bones are best. Olga'll help me, she said." His eyes lit up. "And we could go and see if Fleck's bed has come in. The man in the pet shop said it might be in today."

He bent down to the dog and put his arm around him. "I won't be long, Fleck — and then we'll go into the park and go and see the tree and the drain . . . and maybe Hilary will be there."

Fleck wagged his tail and tried to lick Hal's face, but when Albina spoke sharply to him he whimpered and went to fetch his facecloth. His eyes, as he watched the door close behind Hal, were dark pools of anxiety.

Something was wrong.

• • •

Hal came running in an hour later, already whistling for the dog as he opened the door. "Fleck," he called. "Fleck, I'm back!"

He waited for the yelps of welcome, the sound of toenails skittering over the marble floor of the entrance hall.

Silence.

Olga went to look in the kitchen. Hal raced through the house.

"His leash's gone. That must mean that Mummy's taken him out for a walk. I knew she'd get to like him. I knew it!"

Olga's face was grave.

"I make cocoa" was all she said.

It was nearly an hour before they heard the sound of the car, and then Albina got out. She had no leash, no small white dog . . . only some parcels.

Hal ran toward her. "You've got Fleck, haven't you?"

"No, Hal, I haven't. Fleck's gone back to where he came from."

Hal did not speak, but something had happened to his face that made Albina step back a pace.

"You mean you've taken him back to Easy Pets?"

"Yes, that's right. You see, your father just rented him for the weekend. We could never put up with the inconvenience of a dog for longer than that, but we wanted to give you a treat."

"You're not going to fetch him back?" said Hal in a toneless voice. "It was just a trick you played on me?"

"Not a trick, Hal. We just wanted you to have a dog for a little while. You know how I feel about animals in the house. And I've bought you a present."

She handed him a gaudily wrapped box. The next second the box flew across the room and crashed into a vase on the ornamental chest.

"Oh, Hal, look what you've done," shrieked Albina.

"It's what you've done," said Hal in a strange, grown-up voice. "That's what you want to think about."

And then he turned and went up to his room and shut the door.

7

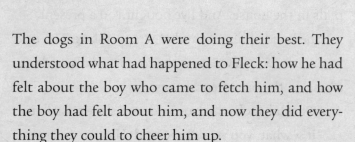

Sorrow

The dogs in Room A were doing their best. They understood what had happened to Fleck: how he had felt about the boy who came to fetch him, and how the boy had felt about him, and now they did everything they could to cheer him up.

All of them had known sorrow. Francine still dreamed of the circus and the busy, useful life she had led there. Honey, in her sleep, still raced over the heather-clad hills at the sound of her master's whistle. Otto had never stopped yearning for the peace of the monastery and the silent dignity of the monks. Li-Chee still waited for someone who would look into his fiery soul.

They had all hoped, as Fleck had hoped, that they would find a master worth serving — and had found only borrowers who came and went and did not care — but they were older and wiser than the little mongrel and they knew that one had to pull oneself together and make the best of things.

Fleck, in his cage, tried desperately to take in what they were telling him, but he was overwhelmed by grief. He lay with his head between his paws. His coat looked dead, his eyes were dull, and he had eaten almost nothing since his return.

Kayley was working in the cubicle next door and whenever she could she came in to look at the Tottenham terrier. She had saved the blue facecloth that had been clamped between Fleck's teeth when he was returned. Mr. Carker would not allow it in the cage, but fortunately the Carkers were away at a dog show looking for exotic dogs to buy and now she dipped it in Fleck's water bowl and moistened his mouth.

"You must try and drink," she told him. "You're still a young dog. This isn't the end of the world."

But she was lying and she knew it. Fleck's world

had ended when the door of his cage shut behind him and Albina Fenton hurried away on her high heels.

"Please, Fleck, for all our sakes," said Kayley, stroking his weary head.

But Fleck only looked at her with his unequal eyes, and gave a desolate whimper, which he quickly tried to repress, because he knew that Mr. Carker did not approve of unhappiness.

Yet the daily round had to go on. Kayley went to hose down the yard, Otto was led away by a weedy man who wanted to impress his friends. Li-Chee went off to sit on the lap of yet another ancient lady . . . and Fleck rolled himself up into a dismal ball at the back of his cage and escaped into sleep.

"Is he any better?" asked Pippa, as soon as Kayley had taken off her coat.

Kayley shook her head. She was very tired.

"But that's ridiculous," said Pippa. "He can't go breaking his heart after only three days with someone. It isn't what happens."

"It has happened," said Kayley, and flopped into a chair.

She wasn't usually like that, and Pippa, who thought the world of her sister, was angry.

"I expect the boy's forgotten all about him," said Pippa.

"No," said Kayley. "He won't have done that. Some boys would have done that but not this one. It was just one of those things."

Ralph, one of the twins, looked up from his homework and said it was like *Romeo and Juliet*. "They only saw each other for a moment on a balcony or something and that was it."

"How did it turn out?" asked Pippa.

"Badly," said Ralph. "Everybody died."

"Idiot!" said Pippa. She could see that Kayley was at the end of her rope. She poured her sister a cup of tea, but Kayley was scowling. Things did happen that were over the top. There was the story of Greyfriars Bobby — a Skye terrier who wouldn't leave his master's grave and lay on his tombstone every night for eight years till he died, too. It was supposed to have really happened — one could go to Edinburgh and see the grave.

"Well, if the boy hasn't forgotten about him, then

he's just feeble. It's because he's rich, I suppose. Rich people are always wimps. I wouldn't let someone give me a dog and then take it away again. Not on your life."

"What could he do?" asked Kayley. "He's only a kid."

"He could steal Fleck," said Pippa. "That's what I'd do. It wouldn't truly be stealing. It would be taking back what belongs to one."

But Kayley, remembering Hal, so small and well behaved beside his overbearing father, didn't think there was much likelihood of that.

"We'll have to leave for work very early on Sunday," she told her sister. "The Carkers will still be away. I must say I'll be glad of your help."

But Pippa meant to do more than just help. She meant to investigate.

"I'm going to ask Dr. Rutherford to come and see Hal," said Albina to her husband. He had just come back from Beijing, where he had done an important deal, and looked surprised.

"Is he ill?" he asked.

Albina looked annoyed. "I told you — he's off his food and he looks thoroughly peaked and he hardly speaks to me. School begins again on Monday. We can't send him back looking like something out of an orphanage."

"Oh well, I suppose it can't hurt to get him checked out," said Donald. "There's been a nasty flu bug around. I sat next to a man on the plane who kept sneezing. I hope I haven't caught anything."

When ordinary people want to see a doctor, they go to the office and wait for their turn, but Albina was too rich to be ordinary, and she had a private doctor who would come and see patients in their houses.

Dr. Rutherford was elderly, with white hair and a pleasant face, and when he had examined Hal he asked Mrs. Fenton to leave him to talk to Hal on his own.

"I can't find anything wrong with you physically," he said to the boy, "though of course if you don't eat, you're going to get steadily weaker."

Hal shrugged. "It doesn't matter," he said. "There's nothing I have to do."

Dr. Rutherford waited. "Nothing?" he said.

"No. Not now."

"But you did have? You did have something to do?"

"Yes."

But he wasn't going to talk to the doctor about Fleck, or the way his parents had betrayed him.

"Well, I'll leave you a tonic," said Dr. Rutherford. He smiled. "That's what doctors do when they can't think of anything else. I think that what's the matter with you is in your mind, but if you don't want to speak about it, I won't force you."

Dr. Rutherford went downstairs and found Albina waiting.

"Well? Did you find anything?"

Dr. Rutherford put on his coat. "No. There is nothing physically wrong," he said. "But there is something wrong just the same. The boy is deeply unhappy. Perhaps you know why this might be so?"

Albina flushed. "No, I don't. Hal has everything a child could possibly need." Then as the doctor looked at her steadily: "There was some fuss about a dog — we rented one for him, and he thought it was here to stay and when we took it back he became quite unmanageable."

"Ah. That would explain it," said Dr. Rutherford. And suddenly there came into his mind the memory of a white bull terrier he had owned as a boy. She had run up the sides of trees and hung off a branch with her teeth, like a piece of washing. When she died of old age he had hidden in the attic and cried for a week. "Well, perhaps there is a way of undoing the damage," he told Albina. "You will have to look into your mind."

But Albina, when he left, did not look into her mind; she looked into the kitchen, where she had to prepare her own lunch because Olga the maid had had the nerve to give notice on the day that Fleck was returned.

"You do bad," she said to her employer. "You do bad thing. I go."

And she had left, even though she had no job to go to and Albina offered her more money if she stayed. Fortunately that afternoon, the three G aunts came to tea, and were shocked to hear of the uselessness of the doctor, coming on top of the impertinence of the maid.

"You know, Albina, I was wondering," said Geraldine. "Have you ever thought of sending Hal away to boarding school? I know you'd miss him, but a change of scene is always a good idea."

"And he does seem to be getting rather spoiled. I mean he's been sulking now for nearly a week," said Glenda. "I tried to tell him that the dog would have forgotten him completely, but I don't think he heard me."

"Of course you'd find it difficult without him," said Gloria. "But it's his good you want to be thinking of. And unless you mean to have another baby to keep him company . . . ?"

Albina shuddered. "Oh no! No, I couldn't go through all that again. The diapers . . . and the screams . . ." She pondered what her friends had said. "I suppose he does need companionship. I'll talk to Donald."

Her husband said it would be very expensive. "Boarding schools cost the earth. But I suppose it would help to build his character. The fuss he's made about this silly dog business doesn't make one very cheerful about his future. If I gave way to my feelings every time I had an important deal to do, where would we be now?"

"Of course I'll miss him," said Albina. "I'll miss him very much. But he's so moody at the moment — and anyway I think we'll be moving to a new house again soon. I've seen a place with a swimming pool in the basement — and a billiard room. Not that we play billiards, but you never know — so that'll keep me very busy."

Donald was not interested in Albina's plans for moving. He was used to shifting house every couple of years, just as he was used to changing his car, and his firm was expanding in the Far East. He'd be away even more, but he was glad that Hal would be somewhere settled.

Every man worth his salt wanted his children to have the best.

8

The Cottage by the Sea

"There's a postcard from Hal," said Alec Fenton, coming into the cottage and stamping the mud off his boots. It was only a few steps to the shore where he kept his dinghy, but it had rained in the night and the path easily turned to mud.

His wife, Marnie, who was kneading bread at the kitchen table, wiped her hands and smiled with pleasure. "Let's have a look, then."

It was a long time since they had been to London to visit Hal's parents, but they thought the world of their grandson.

Marnie read the card over her husband's shoulder.

"Well, that is good news! He's got a dog all for himself! I always said that was what Hal needed."

Alec nodded. "Growing up in that museum — it's no life for a boy."

He looked out of the cottage window. The tide was out, and the sand stretched in a golden curve to the water's edge. It was a quiet day and the islands were distinct: the big island, Farra, where the monks had lived in medieval times, the smaller low-lying island where their neighbor grazed his sheep, and the rocky outcrop where the seals came to breed. A cormorant dived from a rock and came up with a fish in its beak. The gulls circled. Alec's own boat, the *Peggotty*, was pulled up on the shore, ready for the evening's fishing.

"It looks as though Albina's seen the light," said Marnie, "if she's let him have a dog. Maybe we were hasty, thinking ill of her."

The visit that they had paid to Albina and their son had been such a wretched business that they had never gone back. They had been made to feel like the crudest peasants. Albina had raised her eyebrows when she saw their luggage, and said, "Really?" in a surprised voice when they said they'd prefer to sleep together in the one room rather than have the separate rooms she offered them.

"We've been together for thirty-five years," Alec had said. "We've no call to change now."

She had looked pained when Marnie went to the kitchen to thank the maid for the nice meal she had cooked, and pointed out that the maid was paid to do the cooking.

And their own son, Donald, had hardly been there. He was endlessly flying about, and driving about, and when he was at home he had things dangling from his ear the whole time so that he could talk to Moscow or New York instead of the people in the room.

Donald had been a nice, ordinary little boy. He'd helped his father with the lobster pots, and worked in the fields, and they had hoped he would take over the land and the boat when the time came.

But after he'd got a scholarship to a posh boarding school, Donald had changed. He'd made remarks about the cottage, how shabby it was, and how small, and asked why they didn't get a proper car instead of

the wheezing old truck they used for everything —
and he'd gone off to make his fortune in the south.

And he had made it, all right. If living in a house
where the bath taps glittered so much that they gave
you a headache, the food looked as though it was
waiting to be photographed for a magazine, and there
wasn't a living thing in sight was what he wanted, he'd
made it, all right.

But Hal . . . Hal was different. He was the most
loving, funny little boy. Alec and Marnie would have
gathered him up and taken him away on the spot if
they'd been allowed to. Even then they'd seen how
lonely the little fellow was.

But now he'd be better. There was nothing like a
dog for company. They had only their old Labrador
now, but they couldn't imagine life without a dog.

"Let's write him a letter and ask him if he can't
come up to visit us and show us Fleck. Albina must
have changed if she's let him have a dog. If Donald's
too busy to bring him, there might be someone coming north and we could meet him."

So they wrote a letter to Hal, not just a postcard. It
said they hoped he could come now he was older, and

bring his dog. They said it wasn't a difficult journey. If he could get a train as far as Berwick, they would meet him, and after that, it was only half an hour's drive in the truck.

Hal got this letter on the day he went off with his mother to buy clothes for boarding school.

9

Dog Rescue

Mr. Carker put an advertisement for his Easy Pets business into the papers every month. The advertisements were very glossy and there were pictures of the particularly beautiful or rare dogs that could be hired. In the latest advertisement there was a mention of the Tottenham terrier, a new breed of which there were very few specimens in England, and it said that Easy Pets was the first rental agency that had such a dog on its books.

This advertisement was read by a Miss Gertie Gorland, a tall, thin woman who lived with her brother Harold, who was also tall and thin.

The Gorlands ran a hotel by the seaside that was doing badly, and a steam laundry that was doing badly, and a delicatessen that was not only doing badly but had actually gone bust, and when they saw the advertisement they had a brain wave. "We could breed Tottenham terriers," said Gertie. "Set up a puppy farm. If they're so rare, people will pay fortunes for them."

So they went around to Easy Pets and arranged to hire out Fleck for a couple of hours. They wanted to make sure that this new breed was not fierce or liable to attack strangers.

When they saw Fleck they quickly stopped worrying about his fierceness. He was curled up in his cage and scarcely looked up when they came in — there is nothing like misery for making one tired — but when Kayley put on his collar and leash, he followed them dutifully out into the street. To tell the truth, he didn't care whom he was with or where he was going.

The Gorlands hadn't gone far when they decided that the Tottenham terrier was not likely to catch on as a fashionable pet. No one stopped them and asked them where they had got that dear little dog, no heads turned — and out in the strong light they had to admit that the terrier was an odd-looking creature with his short legs and batlike ears.

When they had walked for a while, Gertie said she was hungry, and Harold said he was hungry, too. Tall, thin people need a lot to eat.

"We could see what he's like in crowded places," said Gertie, looking down at the dog.

So they turned into a well-known department store where there was a grand restaurant that permitted one to bring in dogs. The owners had been forced to do this because a lot of famous people ate there who refused to be parted from their pets.

When the waiter had shown them to their table, the Gorlands put the loop of Fleck's leash under the leg of Gertie's chair, and when he had smelled the hundred or so pairs of uninteresting feet and the overrich smells of the food, Fleck crawled under the table and went to sleep.

"I'm not being difficult," said Hal. "It's just that I don't mind whether I have a blue lunch box or a brown one. I would mind if I could, but I can't. It doesn't make any difference."

Albina sighed. "I don't know what to do with you. I'm spending a fortune to make sure you're properly outfitted for your new school, and you just stand there like a dummy."

They were in a famous department store, buying Hal's school uniform for Okelands. They had already bought four pairs of navy blue trousers, six white shirts, two striped ties, and a cap with the Okelands motto on it. The motto was in Latin, and usually Hal would have asked what it meant, but now he didn't care. If it said *Go Out and Kill People with a Hatchet*, it wouldn't have mattered. Nothing mattered to Hal anymore.

After the lunch box came the scarf and the blazer and the socks. . . .

When everything had been paid for, Albina decided to go around the store. Although she didn't need a wedding dress she took Hal through the bridal department, and though she already had eighteen nightdresses she took him through lingerie, and though she never gardened, only got the maid to hose down the gravel, she went through the gardening department, fingering wheelbarrows and tubs of artificial roses.

In the jewelry department she bought herself a diamond bracelet, and after that she was in such a good mood that she said she would take Hal out to lunch in the restaurant that was famous for its exotic and unusual food. Hal had eaten there before and been sick afterward, but he followed his mother and the waiter to a table covered in a pink cloth, with a vase of lilies in the center. The smiling waiters wore tailcoats and an orchestra played softly on a dais.

"Now, isn't this nice," said Albina. She took the huge menu the waiter offered her and became absorbed in it.

"I think we'll have —" she began.

But she didn't go on.

Three tables away, Gertie was just dipping her spoon into her tomato soup when a kind of earthquake hit the store.

The Tottenham terrier who had been lost to the world leapt to his feet and pulled so hard at his leash that Gertie's chair fell over and she went crashing to the floor, followed by the bowl of soup, which landed upside down on her blouse.

And as she lay kicking and screaming, Fleck took off.

This exhausted little dog who had hardly been able to put one foot in front of the other raced across the room like a bullet from a gun, passed the first table — felling a waiter who was carrying a tray of glasses and a bottle — and the second table, where a man tried to catch him and toppled over backward, and crashed violently into the third . . .

. . . where a boy had jumped to his feet, knocking over the vase of flowers, which rolled onto the floor and tripped up a lady making her way to the toilet.

The headwaiter, hurrying in through the double doors from the kitchen to see what had happened, found everyone screaming and complaining and mopping at their clothes. Everyone except a young boy and a small dog, who saw nothing but each other.

"It's absolutely extraordinary," said Albina to her husband when he came home that night. "They had to send for a security guard to carry the wretched dog away, howling and struggling, with his head twisted toward Hal. And yet Hal just sat in the taxi on the way home without any fuss. He didn't cry or anything. And he seems quite resigned to going away to school. He's asked if he can spend the night with Joel tomorrow to say good-bye. That was the friend he made in his first school – do you remember? Rather a common little boy, but I've said yes."

"Well, it looks as though he's growing up at last," said Donald. "We've obviously done the right thing, not letting him wear us down. I'll go and say good night to him."

Going up to his son's room, Donald saw that Albina had been telling the truth. Hal seemed calm and quiet, he hardly mentioned having met Fleck in the restaurant, and he said he was looking forward to going to school and that he was glad to have a chance to say good-bye to Joel.

And indeed Hal was calm and quiet, because he now knew exactly what he was going to do. One of the things that people had told him was that Fleck would have forgotten him. Well, they had been wrong about that and it seemed to him that they were wrong about most of the things that mattered.

Hal was tired of living in a grown-up world. It was time to make his own world where things were right and fair and as they ought to be.

Mr. Carker was in a towering rage. He stamped through his office, cursing and swearing. The restaurant had sent in a huge bill for the damage that the little dog had done. Gertie Gorland was suing him for the price of her blouse, which had been entirely ruined by soup. The businessmen whose suits had been damaged when the waiter's tray fell on them were asking for hundreds of pounds to buy new ones, and the lady who had fallen on her way to the toilet was going to send him her medical bills.

"I won't have it," raged Mr. Carker. "I'll fight everyone. I won't pay a penny to those rogues! As for that blasted dog, he's out of his mind. It's probably inbreeding — you get that in these pedigree animals."

He sent for the vet and told him to give Fleck an injection that would keep him quiet till he decided what to do with him, after which he and Mrs. Carker set off for a nice weekend in Brighton to get over the strain of the last few days. Kayley would see to the dogs on Sunday. She always did.

But on Sunday morning, Kayley woke with a temperature, a sore throat, and a splitting headache.

"You've got the flu," said her mother. "And you're not going to work."

"I have to," said Kayley. "Pippa can't manage everything on her own and she's got all her stuff to get ready."

Pippa was going off to spend a week at school camp on the following day.

But when Kayley tried to sit up in bed, the room spun around and she was forced to lie down again.

"Of course I can manage on my own," said Pippa, looking mulish. "I know exactly what to do and you know it."

"It's too much," Kayley repeated.

But by this time, Pippa was halfway out of the door.

All the same, Kayley was right. There was a terrible lot to do.

On Sundays there were no rentals; the dogs spent the morning in the compound while the rooms were cleaned, the cages swept, the water bowls rinsed out, and the carpets vacuumed. In the afternoon the dogs were taken back to their cages for a couple of hours while the yard was hosed down and the bedding in their sleeping quarters changed and the food prepared.

By four o'clock Pippa was exhausted. There were only the dogs in Room A now to be taken back, and the burglar alarm to be put on and she could go home. Otto and Francine and Honey and the little Peke sat quietly in their cages, but Fleck was stretched out barely conscious after his injection. Pippa had had to carry him in from the compound and she felt such rage that if Mr. Carker had come in then, she would have throttled him. It was for being loving and faithful that the little dog had been punished.

As she bent down to his cage, Pippa heard a noise coming from the office next door. It sounded as though the door from the street was being opened — and by someone who did not want to be heard.

The alarm was not switched on yet. Pippa waited till the sound came again. Then she pounced.

"Got you!" she said, bursting through the door.

The boy she had surprised was about her own age, a slight, fair boy wearing a rucksack and carrying a canvas bag.

Pippa stared. At the same time from next door came the sound of Fleck whimpering in his drugged sleep, and suddenly Pippa knew.

"You're the boy who had Fleck," she said. "Hal, is that your name?" She looked more closely. "Have you come to steal him?"

Hal wasted no time.

"Yes," he said. "And you're not going to stop me."

"I never said I was. But have you got a proper plan?"

Hal nodded. "My parents think I'm staying with a school friend, but I'm going to take the night train to the Scottish border. You can buy a ticket for a dog. I've got money. My grandparents live there. They'll take us in, I know they will."

"Well, that sounds all right. But I warn you, you'll have to carry Fleck at first."

Hal's face went white. "Is he hurt?"

"No. But that charming Mr. Carker ordered him to have an injection to keep him quiet. Come on, we'd better hurry. I've got his facecloth — you'd better take that. Thank goodness my sister's not here. She's one of those good people. She can't help it; she thinks you mustn't break the law."

"I used to be like that," said Hal.

He followed her into the room and bent over Fleck's cage. Hal had no eyes for anyone except Fleck, but the other dogs got to their feet, quivering with curiosity and excitement . . . and then with despair.

For they knew what was going to happen. Fleck's story was going to end happily. His master had returned and was gathering him up to take him out into the world. Fleck was going to be free.

Otto was as devoid of envy as any dog, but his whole body trembled with longing. Francine had pushed her muzzle right up to the bars and her black eyes were full of grief. Grunts of frustration came from the Peke.

Hal, lifting up his sleeping dog, saw none of

this. But Pippa saw it. She had grown up with these dogs and she knew them like she knew her own brothers.

"Let me know when you get there," she said. She scribbled her name and phone number on a piece of paper and Hal put it in his pocket.

"Thank you," he said. "I won't forget."

It was very quiet when Hal had gone. Time to take the other dogs back to the compound and put on the burglar alarm. Time to go home.

But Pippa did not move. She was looking at Otto, still trembling with longing, at the anguish in the collie's eyes. . . .

And she was their jailer. Hal, whom she had despised as rich and feeble, had freed his dog, but not she. She was dooming them to imprisonment, to sitting there like toys, day after day, waiting to be claimed.

The dogs expected nothing. They only looked. Then Otto moaned once softly — and suddenly Pippa went crazy. She marched over to the cages and one by one she undid the catches and threw wide the doors.

Then she opened the door into the office and the one out into the street.

"You can go," she told the dogs.

And they understood her. Otto waited for a moment to lick her hand; Honey rubbed her head against Pippa's skirt, saying thank you.

Then they were gone.

Only Queen Tilly stayed in her cage, though the door was open. Freedom did not interest this spoiled creature. Later she began to complain because her hot water bottle had gone cold, but there was nobody left to hear her. Nobody at all.

10

And Then There Were Five

Hal's arms were getting tired. He had not expected to have to carry his dog to King's Cross station. He had bought a map and learned the route from Easy Pets and it shouldn't have taken more than an hour to walk, but that was when he thought that Fleck would be trotting at his heels.

To begin with, the little dog was just a dead-weight, but now he was beginning to stir in Hal's arms. His back leg twitched once, then again, and Hal turned into a small park with a fountain and sat down on the rim. It was dusk, and the people were all leaving. Soon the streetlights would be lit.

The panic Hal had felt when he found Fleck stretched out in his cage had died down. Pippa had told him that he would recover, and Pippa knew about dogs. Now he laid Fleck down across his lap and began slowly, steadily to stroke his back.

"Please wake up," he begged his dog. "Please."

And it worked. The injection was wearing off and now Fleck turned and opened his eyes — and then he looked at Hal. Looked and looked with his dark right eye and his gold-flecked left eye, trying to believe what he was seeing. He gave a ghost of a whimper and then another. He was still too weak to do more than faintly move his tail, but as he took in that he was really there, where he needed to be, he began carefully to lick Hal's wrist. He licked it steadily and thoroughly, making sure that everything was as clean as it ought to be.

Then he began on the other one. No piece of skin was left unwashed; every inch was cared for. Only when he had made certain that everything was as it should be did his tail start to wag, slowly at first, then fast, and faster . . . and from his throat came a burst of ecstatic barks.

And Hal held him close and told him that he would never leave him again. Never.

"I swear it, Fleck," said Hal to his dog. "No one will come between us ever again, do you hear me?"

Fleck heard him. He became very quiet, and sighed, and buried his head in Hal's chest and slept once more.

At first the four dogs Pippa had let out simply ran. They bounded down the long straight street that led away from Easy Pets, feeling the strength in their legs and the breeze blowing through their coats. Li-Chee had to take four steps to one of theirs, but even with his bandy legs he kept up.

They were free! No one tugged at their leashes, shouted at them, pulled them away from whatever it was that they wanted to see or smell or touch. They had dreamed of running like this so often as they slept, their limbs twitching — and woken to face another day of sitting in their cages.

When they had run the length of the shopping street, they came to a row of houses with yards. One of the garden gates was open. The patch of lawn was messy and rough; there were no flowers in the flower beds. It was exactly right for what they needed to do.

Francine went first, rolling and rubbing and rolling again. Then Honey followed, and Otto and Li-Chee. They rolled and turned and crawled on their stomachs, rubbing themselves as hard as they could against the scratchy grass. They pushed their faces into the earth. From time to time they stopped, their tongues lolling from the effort, and grinned at one another.

And it worked! Gradually the loathsome scents that had been sprayed on the dogs at Easy Pets disappeared, blotted out by earth and grass and moldy leaves and comforting compost. The last whiffs of Mountain Glory left Otto's thick coat, the vile odor of Francine's Dancer coiled up and was wafted away. Honey's horrible Heather Mist and Li-Chee's Lotus Blossom were extinguished. They sniffed one another blissfully, making sure that they smelled as they should smell once again: of dog. But now someone came out of the house, shouting and shooing.

"Get out!" he said. "Get out of my yard at once."

The dogs looked at him. They would have liked to thank him for the use of his yard but he didn't seem to want to be thanked so they trotted out of the gate and into the street.

Now that they were rid of the ghastly, gooey scents that had plagued them, they could really enjoy the smells they came across. Spices from a distant kebab shop . . . pigeons on the roof . . . worm casts in a tub . . . an old shoe caught in a drain . . . dust and the sour smell of spilled milk from a doorway . . . cats that had passed by, of course . . . tomcats, kittens . . . a dead mouse in a gutter . . .

They had never been allowed to spend long enough at a lamppost, with its whirligig of amazing odors, before someone had yanked them back.

Then suddenly Otto stood stock-still and called the others. They came at once because what Otto had discovered was obviously important. They had caught the smell of a hundred pairs of feet, and of more dogs than they could count, but the smell that now came to them was familiar. It belonged to the boy who had come to Easy Pets to take away his dog. Now, as they put their noses together, they could smell the dog. It was Fleck, the small white mongrel who had been their friend.

They waited no longer. Their noses down, their tails up, they set off down the road, across a crosswalk, and into a small park with a fountain.

Everybody now felt fine except for Hal. Fleck had greeted his friends with enthusiasm, barking and wagging his tail from the security of Hal's lap. The four dogs who had been freed from Easy Pets felt fine, too. It was good to see the little terrier again, and though roaming free through the town had been interesting, it was comforting to find a human whom they could trust. They settled themselves at Hal's feet, ready to do his bidding, and Li-Chee, who was really very tired, closed his eyes and had a nap.

But Hal was desperate. He hadn't been able to believe his eyes when the Easy Pets dogs came bounding across the park toward him. What should he do now? The dogs must have escaped after Pippa left, which meant she would get into trouble, but he couldn't think of that now. Nor could he take the dogs back. The risk that there would be someone there who would make him give Fleck back was far too great.

"Go home," Hal said, trying to sound firm. "Go on — go home!" And he waved his arms in the direction of the street.

The dogs just looked at him. Otto's ears twitched; Francine blinked. Humans did make odd remarks like that sometimes. It was best to take no notice. Where was home? Certainly not the place they had come from. Not one of them moved.

And why should they, thought Hal. What kind of "home" was Easy Pets for a self-respecting dog? But he had to get Fleck to King's Cross. The train left at nine-thirty and it was the last one of the night. Surely if he began to walk, they would make their own way?

He put Fleck down on the ground, and clipped on his collar and leash. It was awful to leave the dogs to fend for themselves, but he had to get Fleck away before anyone noticed that he was gone.

He began to walk toward the gates of the park. Fleck could walk quite well now, with only a slight drunken lurch. The effects of the injection were almost gone. And a few paces behind, quietly and without fuss, came Otto and Francine, Honey and Li-Chee. A drunk carrying a bottle came toward them, and Otto's hackles rose. He growled in his throat, and the drunk retreated. Not only was Otto accompanying them, but he had set himself up as a bodyguard.

Following his map, Hal walked the streets of London with his Tottenham terrier — and a few paces behind, correct and obedient, came the four dogs who had broken free. Every so often Hal stopped and said, "Go home, go on. Go!" and they looked at him politely, waiting till he should set off again. They were no trouble, stopping at crosswalks, talking to any other dogs they met only briefly before catching up again with Hal. Fleck's tail was high with pride, for not only was he reunited with his master, but he was enjoying the company of his friends.

They reached King's Cross at last. Fleck was overwhelmed by the throng of people, and Hal picked him up as he made his way to the ticket office.

"Go home, please," he said for the last time to the four dogs who were following him, but they only pressed closer on his heels because there were smells and sounds there that were most unappealing to self-respecting dogs. Someone was being sick; a group of people in funny hats were shouting and hiccuping and singing stupid songs. The dogs looked at Hal with their innocent eyes, wondering why they were there, but they trusted him to do his best even in this loathsome place.

Hal was desperate. He carried Fleck to the line for the ticket office, and the four dogs lined up also, silent and well behaved. Even if he'd had the money to buy tickets for the four escapees, he couldn't have done it. The regulations said a passenger was allowed to bring only one dog onto the train.

"Yes?" said the ticket clerk impatiently.

"A single to Berwick on Tweed and one for the dog," said Hal, laying his money on the counter.

He took his ticket and the one for Fleck. The train was on platform seven. There weren't many trains now. He made his way along the almost empty platform, and the dogs, full of trust, came after him.

Hal knew there was only one thing to do. Getting Fleck away safely was a matter of life and death. He would get on the train and shut the door quickly and then — he was sure — the other dogs would go away. In the morning, when he reached Berwick, he would ring Pippa and tell her what had happened and she could organize a search for the dogs. Nothing terrible could happen to them in one night.

He put Fleck down on the floor of the carriage. Then he climbed in after him and turned to shut the door. The four dogs were still on the platform, looking up at him trustingly, but he hardened his heart.

"Come on, Fleck," he said, and made his way to his seat.

"The nine-thirty P.M. service for Berwick and Edinburgh is now ready to depart from platform seven," said a voice over the loudspeaker.

Doors slammed shut. The guard gave his signal. The train began to move.

The phone went at six o'clock in the morning and Pippa ran into the hall and lifted the receiver. It would probably be from Alison, the friend she was meeting so they could go to school together. Everybody was assembling there to wait for the bus that would take them to the camp in the New Forest.

But it was not Alison.

"Is that Pippa?" said a faint voice.

"Yes. Who's that?"

"It's Hal."

"Goodness! Have you got to your grandparents' already?"

"No, I haven't." Hal's voice sounded strained and worried. "I'm still here. I'm in London because an awful thing's happened. All the dogs that were in the room with Fleck have escaped, and they caught up with me and won't go away. I'd got on the train, I was all ready to go, but they just sat on the platform and looked and waited. They were sure I was going to take them, too. I tried to ignore them but I couldn't, so I got off the train again and spent the night in a freezing shed at the back of a building site. It was horrible. There was a Rottweiler guarding it, but Otto just talked to him and he let us in. Only you've got to come and take the dogs back, Pippa. You've got to."

Pippa's mind was racing. "Where are you? Tell me exactly."

"I'm in Mortland Square. There's a patch of grass and a war memorial. I can wait here for a while, but people are beginning to stare. It's off the North Road."

"All right. I know it. Just stay there. Don't move, whatever you do. Tell them you're waiting for their owners or something."

She put down the phone. Kayley was still asleep. She'd been asleep the previous night, too, when Pippa came back. Pippa's rucksack was packed, there was only her toothbrush to put in and the bag of sandwiches her mother had made the night before. She crept to the kitchen and took it from the fridge and added some cold sausages and half a loaf of bread. Then she hurried to the sitting room and turned on the computer and printer and wrote a note to her teacher to say that she had the flu and would be unable to come to camp, and signed it with her mother's name. Her mother's handwriting was easy to copy.

"Did I hear the phone?" said Mrs. O'Brian sleepily as Pippa crept in to say good-bye.

"Yes. It was Alison to say we're to meet half an hour earlier. I'll have to be off."

She hugged her mother and let herself out of the house. When she reached Alison's house she dropped the letter in and hurried on to the bus stop. She was sorry to miss the camp, but Hal was obviously going to make a thorough mess of things if she didn't get there to put him right.

Hal looked cold and peaked and there was a smutty stain on his cheek, but the dogs seemed to be in fine fettle. They greeted her rapturously, tails rotating like windmills. Francine gave her a paw; Honey rubbed her nose against Pippa's leg.

Pippa opened her rucksack.

"We'd all better eat something," she said. "Cold sausages aren't good for dogs, but they'll have to do."

The sausages did very well, wolfed down by all five of the dogs, and Pippa and Hal shared the sandwiches. Hal was beginning to feel a bit better. The night on the filthy floor of the hut had taken it out of him.

"We'll get a hot drink in a minute," said Pippa. And then: "I think I better tell you what happened to the dogs. They didn't escape. I let them out. On purpose."

Hal stared at her. She went on. "Suddenly I couldn't bear to see them in their cages like that, when Fleck was going to be free. It was a sort of brainstorm, I suppose. Really stupid. Anything could have happened to them, but it didn't. They found you so that's all right."

"But it isn't all right," said Hal frantically. "I must get away. I think I may be able to change my ticket — I'm not sure — but I can't take the others. You simply have to take them back."

"Well, I'm not going to," said Pippa firmly, zipping up the rucksack, "so you can forget that absolutely."

Fleck was in his usual position on Hal's lap and Hal gathered him and held him very close.

"My parents will find I'm gone in a few hours and then it will all begin. And I tell you if they try to take Fleck away again, I'll kill them, and no one wants to kill their parents."

"Never mind your parents," said Pippa. "What about your grandparents? The people you're escaping to. What are they like? Describe them."

"They're very kind and . . . quiet but not soft at all. They're like . . . it sounds silly, but like trees, or

114

earth . . . things that are just there and you don't think about them, but it would be awful if they were gone."

"And you're sure that they'd take you in, you and Fleck?"

"Yes. They've always thought I should have a dog and they live by the sea in Northumberland where there's lots of space. They wouldn't just send us back, I'm sure."

Pippa was fiddling with the strap of her rucksack. Otto had come to sit beside her and was resting his head on her shoulder. "And what about the others?" She waved her hand at the four dogs sitting around in a companionable silence. "Would they take them in, too?"

This was difficult. "I don't know," said Hal slowly. "They live in a small cottage and my parents are always saying how poor they are . . . but I don't believe they'd send the dogs back to Easy Pets once they knew what it was like. I don't know, but I don't believe they would."

"Well, that settles it," said Pippa. "We'll come with you. We'll all go to Northumberland."

Hal stared at her. "But how? I've hardly any money left and they won't let us take all the dogs on the train."

"Then we won't go by train. We'll walk and get lifts on trucks or on anything we can get to take us. You'll see," said Pippa, getting to her feet. "We'll get a map as soon as the shops open. But it can't be too difficult. After all, one thing is certain about Northumberland. It must be in the north."

11

Hal Has Gone

Albina was sitting by the telephone. She was as pale as death and every so often she let out a little moan. Gloria sat beside her, ready to take over when Albina had to go to the lavatory so that the phone was never left unattended. Geraldine was manning the coffee machine in the kitchen.

The Fentons were waiting for word from the kidnappers who held Hal. Any moment now they would call and demand an enormous ransom for the boy — and then Hal would be returned. Donald had sent out for thousands of pounds in cash. It was in a pouch in the hall guarded by Glenda so that they could drive it instantly to wherever the kidnappers wanted to meet them.

If they were willing to pay enough, Hal would be returned, they told themselves again and again. Everything would surely come right, if the money was there. Even in their distress and fear for Hal, the Fentons found it hard to believe that money wasn't the answer to everything.

It was three hours now since they had called Joel's parents to tell them to send Hal home, and heard that Hal had not been with them — that they had no idea where he was.

Albina's terrified shriek had brought Donald running, and half an hour later the house filled with policemen. Donald had been angry because they were ordinary constables, not high-ranking detectives, and he'd made so much fuss that a second squad car arrived with an inspector and a superintendent.

The police had searched the house, examined Hal's belongings, taken photographs, and removed items from the bathroom for DNA testing.

And they had asked questions, some of which had annoyed the Fentons very much.

"Is there anything that was upsetting your son?" they had wanted to know. "Anything that might make him think of running away?"

Even in the midst of their grief, Hal's parents had been very angry.

"Certainly not. Hal had everything a boy could want," said Albina.

"You say he was going away to boarding school. Could he have been frightened of that?"

"No. Definitely not." Both Hal's parents were certain. "He said only yesterday how much he was looking forward to it. And you can see," repeated Albina, waving her hands at the heaped-up toys in Hal's room, "he had everything a boy could want. He wouldn't run away."

"I tell you the boy's been kidnapped," said Donald. "Everyone knows we're well off. You must get a lead on that — and make it clear that we'll pay any ransom. The sky's the limit."

But the infuriating policemen had insisted on going through the routine procedures and getting the names of all the people they wanted to question: Joel's parents, Hal's school friends, people in the shops.

"Was there anyone else working here in the house?" asked the superintendent.

"There was a maid, a foreigner. But she won't know anything. Unless she's in league with the kidnappers. She was a most impertinent woman."

A policeman took down Olga's address. His slowness infuriated Donald.

"For God's sake! Surely you know how to track down kidnappers? They're probably a well-known gang. They could be hacking off his ear." He broke off and turned his head away. All the ghastly things he had seen on television swam before him. "I'll offer a hundred thousand pounds' reward for any information," he went on. "Make sure you put that up everywhere."

"Best hold on a minute, sir. We don't want everybody coming in with cock-and-bull stories. Not till we've finished our inquiries."

So now they had gone, leaving Donald desperate and fuming.

"They're hopeless. You can tell. It's all plod, plod. I'm going to hire a private detective. Mackenzie had one when his wife lost her jewels. He said he was very professional. Cost the earth, but that's all to the good. You can't get the best on the cheap."

Donald went to look up the names of private detectives, and poor Albina sat by the telephone, weeping and waiting for word from the kidnappers while Gloria and Glenda and Geraldine made coffee and brought her clean handkerchiefs. But the hours passed and no word came.

The first thing Kayley heard when she came down the street toward the Easy Pets building was Queen Tilly screaming.

"Oh heavens, what's happened?" said Kayley, and began to run.

She was still ill and shouldn't have been coming to work at all. Her mother had tried to stop her but without success: There was no one else to see to the dogs.

The side door that led into her office was unlocked. The burglar alarm was off.

Kayley's heart was thumping now. What was Queen Tilly doing in her daytime cage when she should have been asleep with the others out in the compound at the back? And why were the doors of the other cages wide open?

Queen Tilly, seeing her, screamed even louder. Her hot water bottle had been cold for hours and she had an itch on her back. Tilly never scratched her own back; she waited till somebody came and gave her a body rub.

But today, Kayley, who always spoke so gently to the dogs, just said, "Shut up, for goodness' sake," and hurried out to the yard. What had happened to the other dogs in Room A? Where were Otto and Francine and Li-Chee and Honey? And where was Fleck?

It didn't take long for her to find out that the dogs were gone. She searched the sleeping quarters, the other rooms, every nook and cranny of the Easy Pets building, whistling and calling, but there was no sign of them.

An hour later, Mr. and Mrs. Carker sat in their office, scowling at the policemen who had come to investigate, and scowling at Kayley.

"It's a tragedy. An outrage," said Mr. Carker. "Five of my most valuable dogs stolen! What do I pay for if not the protection of the police, eh? Tell me that!"

Kayley sat scrunching her handkerchief into a ball. She had been crying and looked completely exhausted, and the youngest of the policemen glanced at her and shook his head.

She had answered their questions as truthfully as she could, but she had not told them everything. It was clear to her that Pippa had forgotten to put on the burglar alarm and as a result the thieves had been able to get in and steal the dogs. And she would not give Pippa away. Her sister was too young to be in that kind of trouble.

"I must have forgotten," she said when she was questioned about the alarm. "I wasn't feeling very well." The police could see that this was true. The girl shouldn't have been at work at all.

But Mr. Carker was busy telling the superintendent how valuable the dogs were.

"The Saint Bernard was bred specially for me in Switzerland," lied Mr. Carker. "He must be worth a cool three thousand pounds. And the poodle won best in show in Paris. I've refused a fortune for her. Every dog in that room is priceless. One of them was a new breed, a Tottenham terrier. He's just been registered by the Kennel Club. I've had a stampede of people trying to buy him off me, but I wouldn't sell."

The policeman who had been recording what Mr. Carker said looked up. "What about that bald little yelper?" he asked. "The Mexican hairless? She was in the same room as the others, wasn't she? Is she worth anything?"

"I'll say she is," said Mr. Carker. "She's the most valuable one of the lot."

"I wonder why they didn't take her, then," said the inspector — and the youngest policeman, who had met Queen Tilly, grinned and said under his breath, "I could guess why not."

Routine investigations took up the next couple of hours — fingerprints, paw marks, door locks, statements. . . .

"We'll let you know, sir," the superintendent said to Mr. Carker. "And we could take the young lady home. She obviously isn't well."

"Oh no, no," said Kayley. "I've got a lot to do."

But when the police had gone, Mrs. Carker turned to her. "I'm afraid you'll lose your job over this. We can't have someone so careless in charge of thousands of pounds' worth of dogs."

Kayley looked at her with brimming eyes. She could not imagine life without the dogs.

But Mr. Carker gave his wife a look. Kayley was paid half of what they would have to pay anybody else. And all the stolen dogs were heavily insured. He wasn't going to lose any money, and that was all that mattered.

"You can stay till we find someone to take your place," he said.

So Kayley went on working though she was ill, though her heart felt like breaking when she thought of the five dogs who had been her friends, and though she was worried sick about Pippa, who would be in such terrible trouble if the truth came out.

Just as the awful day was coming to an end, Donald decided to ring his father and mother up in Northumberland. After all, they were Hal's grandparents. They had a right to know.

Alec and Marnie were already in bed when the phone rang, but Alec padded downstairs, stepped over old Meg, the Labrador, and picked up the phone. He hated the telephone, and a call late at night could only be unwanted news.

But it was worse than he could have imagined.

"Hal's been kidnapped?" he repeated — and took a deep breath because the room was spinning round.

Donald told him what had happened.

"The police think he might have run away, but that's complete nonsense, of course. I've got the name of a detective to put on the case. He's supposed to be very good. He ought to be at that price."

"How's Albina taking it?"

"Badly, of course. She won't go to bed, just sits by the phone."

"Poor lass. You'll let us know the minute you hear anything, won't you?"

"Of course."

Donald was about to hang up when his father asked one more question. "Was the dog with Hal when he disappeared?"

"What dog?"

"Fleck. He wrote us he had a dog."

"No, no. That was days ago. We took the dog back. It was only out on hire. Hal didn't mind. He made a fuss at first and then he forgot all about him. He was excited about going away to school."

Alec went upstairs very slowly. He thought about saying nothing to Marnie, but he'd never been much good at concealing things from his wife.

"What is it?" she asked. "Come on, it's bad news, I know."

Alec told her.

"Donald is sure the boy's been kidnapped, but I wonder."

They sat up in bed, very close together, trying to bear what seemed to be unbearable — that Hal was missing and in danger.

"What exactly did Donald say?" Marnie wanted to know.

She listened carefully while Alec repeated his conversation with their son.

"Well, there's one thing in all that that's nonsense," said Marnie. "There's no way Hal has forgotten about the little dog."

"That's what I thought," said Alec.

After a while they gave up all attempt at sleeping and went downstairs and made a pot of tea. They sat with it while the night turned gradually paler, thinking about the boy they saw so rarely and loved so much. And old Meg lay with her head resting on Alec's feet and kept watch also.

12

The Murgatroyd Family Wedding

The children had walked for several hours and it seemed as though London would never end. They were no nearer a road where trucks might slow down and give them a lift. Hal had had no sleep and very little food. He was completely exhausted, and even Pippa was secretly wondering if they should give up.

They reached a big gas station with a café attached. It was part of a concourse and was completely jammed with a row of cars and trucks and trailers that seemed to belong together.

The children flopped down on a bench by a messy ornamental pool and the dogs had a drink. From the trucks and trailers came unexpected noises — the stamping of hooves, the sound of a parrot squawking, snatches of music. On some of the trailers were red circles and a picture of a clown's head. Scrawled on the sides were the names of the places they were going to: Todcaster, Berwick, Aberdeen. . . . And above them, in big letters: *Henry's Circus for Today*.

"Why is it a Circus for Today?" Hal wondered, and Pippa said it was because they were only allowed to have animals that did tricks anyway, like dogs and horses, not lions or tigers or sea lions.

"They tried having circuses without any animals at all but no one went to them so they brought back all the animals that are tame already."

Wandering between the caravans were gaily dressed people, and mechanics in grease-stained overalls. A woman in a red shawl carried a baby in her arms. Now there was a sort of stirring and everyone began to go back to their cars or caravans. The circus, it seemed, was getting ready to move on.

It was at this moment that they noticed that Francine was missing.

It was an awful moment. The dogs had kept

together throughout the journey; the children had hardly needed to check where they were. Now, though they called and searched, the poodle was nowhere to be seen.

"Find her," said Pippa to the other dogs. "Come on, Otto, you're a rescue dog. Find Francine."

The dogs put their heads down. It was difficult with so many smells coming from the parked vehicles, not to mention fumes from the gas pumps. Then Otto took off toward a trailer parked near the end of the row and galloped around to the other side. They all followed him — and stopped dead.

At first they just thought they were seeing double. There was not one black poodle on the grassy verge, there were two. The second poodle was black like Francine and clipped in the same way — he could have been her twin — but as they stared they saw that he was slightly bigger, and a male.

But it was what the two dogs were doing that made them gaze with open mouths.

The dogs were dancing. Not tottering about on their hind legs as dogs sometimes do, but properly, beautifully dancing to the sound of an accordion played by a tall man in overalls. They pirouetted, they turned, they looked into each other's eyes, held by the music. The big male poodle was absorbed, but Francine was transformed; her eyes shone, her head tilted to catch every drop of sound. They could see how happy she was, how exactly where she wanted to be.

The man put down the accordion and picked up a hoop that had been lying on the grass and held it up. He was a big man; the hoop was high. The male poodle went first, flying through it effortlessly. Then, without a moment's hesitation, Francine followed.

Even in midair, with her ears blown back by the breeze, she seemed to be smiling with pleasure.

But now the man had caught sight of them.

"Well, well," he said, "that's one of the best-trained dogs I've seen. She's got the measure of Rupert all right. I didn't have to tell her anything; she just took off. Looks as though she was trained by Elsa. You can always tell Elsa's dogs; they've got that natural look."

Pippa nodded. "Yes, that's right," she said, to Hal's amazement.

"And this'll be her new act?" said the man, looking at the other dogs. "Trust Elsa to train a Saint Bernard; they hate the noise and fuss of a circus usually. But Elsa could train a brain-dead earthworm. You traveling with her?"

"Yes. She's our aunt. Well, sort of . . ." said Pippa, while Hal continued to stare at her.

The man grinned. "'Sort of' is right — she must be on her fifth husband. But what's she doing here? Last time I heard she was doing the season in Bournemouth."

"I'm afraid that fell through," said Pippa.

"Oh, it did, did it? Well, that's a piece of luck for us. We need a dog act. Petroc's Poodles have let us down — Petroc's had to go to the hospital. I'm just looking after Rupert here till he gets back." He gestured to the poodle standing very close to Francine. "But where's Elsa's van? I didn't see it come in."

"It broke down," said Pippa. "There was a sort of horrible scraping noise. Elsa wasn't at all pleased."

"I bet she wasn't. Swearing fit to bust, I'll wager."

"Yes, she was. She told us to come on ahead and tell you."

"Did she, then?" said the man, whose name was George. "Well, we're just off. You'd better jump in that truck over there for now. There's plenty of room and it's full of hay. We'll sort you out when we get there. Wait till I tell Mr. Henry — he'll be over the moon, Elsa's dogs falling into his lap like that."

He had a word with the driver and let down the tailgate. The children climbed aboard and so did the dogs — except for Francine, who stood still and looked at Rupert, while Rupert looked at her.

"Come on, Francine," called Pippa.

But the two poodles just stood very close together and did not move.

"All right, you can go with them," said George to Rupert, and the two dogs jumped in together and lay down side by side.

"How can you tell all those lies?" asked Hal when they were under way. "You must be crazy."

"They're not lies," said Pippa. "They're stories."

"I can't see the difference," said Hal.

"That's silly! If you're reading a book with people having adventures, you don't think you're reading a lot of lies. You're just glad there's something going on."

Hal was not reassured. Elsa with her five husbands and her bad language sounded absolutely terrifying.

"I expect she carries a whip and cracks walnuts with her teeth," he said.

But, as Pippa pointed out, they were driving steadily in just the direction that they wanted to go.

"Todcaster's only thirty miles south of Berwick. You said nothing mattered except getting Fleck to your grandparents, and that's exactly what we're doing."

And she leaned back against a hay bale and closed her eyes and went to sleep.

It was almost dark before they reached Todcaster, the first town in which the circus was to perform. It was an industrial town surrounded by moorland and as the children tumbled out of the truck they could feel the slight chill in the air, which meant that they were truly in the north.

George was with them almost straightaway.

"Haven't heard anything from Elsa, have you?" he asked, and Pippa said no.

"Aunt Elsa doesn't believe in mobile telephones

because she read somewhere that they give you canker of the ear."

George shook his head. "Daft as a brush; she always was. Still, we need a dog act and hers will be the best. I suppose we'd better fix you up with somewhere to sleep in case she doesn't make it till morning. The dogs can sleep in the truck, but you'll want somewhere a bit more comfortable."

He went off and came back with a nice round-faced woman whom he introduced as Myra.

"She's got a big trailer. You can bunk with her just for one night."

"That's right. There's room for two little ones," said Myra. "We brought up four kids in our camper."

It turned out that Myra was a fortune-teller. When the circus came to rest she smartened up her trailer and put on her hooped earrings and her purple head scarf and told people what was going to happen to them. She called herself Mystic Myra and was very popular because she never told people anything nasty.

"It's not that I believe in it," she told the children. "It's a load of codswallop if you ask me, but it does no harm and every little bit helps where money's concerned."

Myra's husband was called Bill. He'd been a sword swallower, but one day when he was doing his act, two swords had become crossed in his insides and he'd been rushed off to the hospital to have an operation. Now he helped George, who was the chief mechanic.

Bill and Myra couldn't have been friendlier. They cooked a lovely corned beef hash for the children and showed them where they would sleep and even found enough scraps for the dogs, who settled down for the night in the truck. All except Fleck. The Tottenham terrier had tried to keep quiet, but when he realized that Hal was not coming he began to whine and then to shiver — and even though the others looked at him reproachfully, he couldn't stop himself from howling dismally. Ever since Albina Fenton had tried to tear the facecloth from his mouth and carried him back to Easy Pets, Fleck lived in a world where nothing and nobody was safe.

In the trailer, Hal heard him and put down his knife and fork.

"I'm sorry," he said, feeling embarrassed. "He's very young. . . ."

"Oh well, you'd better bring him in, then," said Myra good-naturedly. "I reckon he's not much more than a pup. Though what Elsa would say, spoiling him like that . . ."

So Fleck was brought in and curled up at Hal's feet with his facecloth and fell instantly asleep.

The following day was spent getting everything ready for the performance on the next day. To Hal and Pippa, who had never seen a circus, let alone traveled with one, everything was exciting and amazing. The big top seemed to go up in an instant. . . . One minute there were great folds of canvas lying on the ground, and the next moment the huge dome went up, the flag on the top unfurled to say *Henry's Circus for Today* — and they were in business! They had borrowed leashes for all the dogs so that they could wander about without getting in the way, and wherever they looked there was something going on. The liberty horses, coming out of their vans and stepping across to the stables, the acrobats warming up on mats outside, the clowns unpacking their gear . . .

They watched and wondered, trying to keep out of the way. Otto alone didn't care for what was going on. He was descended from the great Barry, a Saint Bernard who had saved so many people from the snow that when he died he had been stuffed and put in a museum. When you have an ancestor like that, the noise and glitter of a circus are hard to bear, and he plodded along with a weary look in his bloodshot eyes. Li-Chee snuffled along behind him, his long hair brushing the ground, and from time to time he sneezed the fringe out of his eyes. But Francine's feet scarcely touched the grass. She almost danced; her eyes shone. If ever there was a dog who was exactly where she belonged, it was the poodle — and Rupert never left her side.

But now George called them into his camper and asked again if they had heard from Elsa.

"Mr. Henry's waiting for his dog turn. Can you get them to do something without her?"

"We could try," said Pippa. "But it's always Elsa who sets them off. We just watch."

"Well, you think," said George. "We open tomorrow, and if there's no sign of Elsa, we'd better be sending you back. Can't have children gallivanting all over the countryside on their own."

"Could we have a little time to think about it?" asked Pippa. George said yes, they could.

"What are we going to do?" said Hal, as he and Pippa made their way back to the trailer. "We can't possibly make them do tricks."

"We've come such a long way," said Pippa. "If they send us back now, you know what will happen. The dogs back in their cages forever — Fleck, too — and the police probably . . . I don't think I can bear it. There must be something we can make them do."

Myra was tidying the trailer, getting it ready for people who wanted to have their fortunes told. "Petroc's Poodles used to do a turn jumping on and off the backs of the liberty horses as they galloped round the ring," she said. "But I suppose your dogs wouldn't do that."

And the children, remembering the lordly horses with their silken manes, said no, their dogs probably wouldn't do that.

"Well, what's Elsa's show, then? Is it The Murgatroyd Family Go to Their Wedding? I always liked that, with the dogs in their cart on the way to the church. People may say it's old-fashioned but it always goes down well, especially with a bit of business from the clowns."

"Yes," said Pippa, "that's what it is . . . sort of."

"That shouldn't be too difficult, then. If Elsa doesn't get here in time, you could borrow some of Petroc's stuff. He left it all in his van. There'll be a cart of some kind you can use and a hamper full of costumes. I'll get it out for you."

An hour later, the children and the dogs were standing at the entrance to the circus ring. Two of the clowns, Tom and Fred, had found Petroc's cart and Myra had dragged out his dressing-up hamper and gone back to her caravan.

"Well, we'll leave you to get on with it," said Tom. "Just call us when you're ready and we'll fit our business in with you. Then we can have a proper run-through."

They went off. Hal opened the hamper and looked at the gaudy clothes with disgust.

"What gives people the right to dress up animals and make them look as silly as they are themselves?" he asked.

Pippa did not answer, and when Hal looked at her he saw that her face was rigid and she was as pale as death.

"I can't," she gulped, staring at the empty expanse of sawdust, and the rows of tiers stretching upward. "I've absolutely no idea what to do. I must have been crazy."

"But we've said —"

"I can't," said Pippa again. "I absolutely can't." She was almost crying. "We'll have to come clean. I'm very sorry."

The dogs had been waiting patiently, wondering what was going on. Now Francine stepped forward. She dived into the hamper, picked up a wreath of white flowers in her mouth, and laid it on the ground.

"She must have done this before," said Pippa.

They put the wreath over the poodle's head and she sat up on her hind legs, every inch a bride. If Pippa did not know what to do, Francine quite clearly did.

After that, somehow, they managed to carry on. They found a tiny bonnet for Li-Chee, who was to be the baby, and a frilled hat for Honey, who was to be the mother. But Otto took one look at his hat and turned away.

"We can't make him dress up — not Otto," said Hal.

"We won't have to," said Pippa, "not if he's just pulling the cart."

Rupert, of course, was the bridegroom. There was no trouble about getting him to put on a bow tie and a silk waistcoat. He, like Francine, knew that dressing up was part of the job.

They decided that Otto should pull the cart around the ring twice, with Francine and Li-Chee and Honey on board. They would stop at the church, which the clowns would set up, and Rupert would be sitting there, waiting for his bride. The wedding would take place out of sight behind a curtain, and then the bridal party would come out again and drive to the wedding banquet in another part of the ring and the show would end with the two poodles dancing together.

"That part will work at least," said Pippa. "There can be a spotlight on them, and then it can go out suddenly and everything will be over."

But even such a simple routine was unbelievably difficult for the dogs to learn. Getting Otto to pull the cart around the ring took ages. He trembled with outrage, but Pippa was patient. Gradually he went around; his eyes were full of despair, but he went. Li-Chee grumbled in his throat but when Pippa said, "Please, Li-Chee, please," he sat still in his seat. Honey looked around from under her frilled hat as if asking why this was happening to her, but she, too, sat where they put her. Francine, standing straight on top of the cart, kept the other dogs in check.

But Fleck wouldn't leave Hal.

"It's no good. He'll have to stay with you," said Pippa.

Hal agreed, but sadly. "He was such a joyful dog when I first got him," he said. "But now . . ."

"He'll be joyful again, you'll see," said Pippa. "He's just lost his confidence."

They rehearsed for most of the morning, and then the clowns came back. Whatever they thought privately about The Murgatroyd Family Go to Their Wedding, they kept it to themselves.

"We'll come on first, getting the feast ready, trying to blow up balloons and all that," said Tom. "There's plenty of chance there for a bit of business — that'll loosen everybody up. And we'll have a word with Steve about the music. You'll want the wedding march where they go into the church, I expect, and then a waltz when the poodles do their dance."

"Yes," said Pippa. "Thank you. I hope it'll be all right."

Fred looked at her worried face.

"Of course it'll be all right," he said. "And anyway, with a bit of luck Elsa'll be here in time to put on the finishing touches."

The children looked at each other.

It wouldn't need a *bit* of luck for Elsa to come and do that — it would need rather a lot.

13

The Detective Agency

Curzon Montgomery sat in his leather armchair leafing through the pages of *Yachting World*. There was a hundred-foot ketch for sale that he had his eye on. They were asking a ridiculous price, but if the morning's interview went as he hoped, he'd be able to make a bid for it. Not that he liked being at sea. All that roughness and choppiness could really get you down, but you couldn't beat a yacht as a place for giving parties.

The room he sat in did not look like an office. It was furnished like a very expensive sitting room with deep upholstered sofas, a thick-pile carpet, and the kind of pictures on the wall that might be absolutely anything. All the same, it was from this room that Curzon ran his Media Management and Manhunting agency — or MMM for short.

Curzon did not accept just any sort of client, as he made clear. He was very particular — but actually only very special clients could afford his fees. Not that he was greedy, not at all, but his uncle, Lord Featherpool, had invested a lot of money in MMM and he expected results.

Now Curzon rang for his receptionist, and a beautiful girl with a bandage around her ankle came teetering in. Fiona Enderby-Beescombe had been at school with Lord Featherpool's niece and in need of a job, and Curzon had been glad to take her on. It was true that her habit of wearing ten-inch heels meant that she was frequently injured, and she spent so much time painting her fingernails that she did not always reach the phone in time, but Curzon had been pleased to hire her because as soon as she opened her mouth people knew that she came from the right background.

"I'm expecting an important client in ten, Fiona. A Mr. Fenton. We shall want coffee. You'd better turn on the infrared detector and the digital decoder and all that stuff. He might want to have a look. And tell Sprocket to keep out of the way."

Ten minutes. Was there time for a small snifter? A whisky before an interview often made things go smoothly. But before he could open the drinks cabinet, the bell rang and Donald Fenton was shown in.

Donald and Albina had had a sleepless night. The kidnappers had not rung and the police were useless — plodding and slow. But the headquarters of the MMM agency was a reassuring sight. The office was on the most expensive block in the city, the sign outside the door in gold letters so small and discreet that it had taken Donald several minutes to find it. Everything, in short, was of the best.

Curzon rose from his chair. His large red face was amiable. As they shook hands he said, "Now, how can I help you? I gather your son is missing."

"Yes. Yes." Donald was a sorry sight. There were dark rings under his eyes; his hands shook. "We're sure he's been kidnapped, but there's been no word. The police had the nerve to suggest he might have run away, but that's nonsense. Hal had everything he wanted in the world. My wife and I tried to gratify every whim of his. You should see the toys in his nursery."

"Quite. Quite so. Now if you'll just tell me the whole story."

So Curzon switched on the recorder and Donald told of the night they thought Hal had gone to stay with his friend and the awful discovery that he had never turned up there, while Curzon nodded his head in an understanding sort of way.

"I came to you because I heard how you found Mackenzie's wife's diamonds. It was an amazing piece of work," said Donald.

Curzon smirked modestly. "Yes . . . yes. That took a bit of doing. A very tricky case . . . but it came out all right in the end."

Actually what had happened to Mackenzie's wife's diamond necklace was not quite what Curzon pretended. A few days after the necklace went missing, Curzon went around to a cocktail party at the Mackenzies' house and drank so much that he wandered out into the garden to look for a place where he could be sick. He had decided on the compost bin and was just lifting the lid when he saw the glint of diamonds inside. (Mrs. Mackenzie was a keen gardener and had been cutting roses before she set off for the opera.)

So Curzon slipped the necklace into his pocket and two days later he rang Mackenzie and told him that after a very difficult and secret piece of detection he had managed to find it.

"I've brought the photos of Hal, of course, and . . ." — here Donald's voice faltered — "his toothbrush for DNA samples and a few clothes . . ." He turned away to gather himself together.

"Good man. Good . . . Now perhaps you'd like Miss Enderby-Beescombe to show you around the laboratory. As you'll see, we have all the latest equipment. Meanwhile I'll get on to my team."

Although Miss Enderby-Beescombe was a little vague about some of the gadgets she showed him, the hum and whir and flashing lights in the adjoining room were impressive. But what impressed Donald most of all was the fee that MMM charged.

It was six hundred pounds an hour, Curzon told

him, and then a fee of fifty thousand once the boy was found.

Donald, returning home, was able to reassure and comfort Albina. At that price, MMM had to be not only good, but the best.

When Donald had left, Curzon picked up the internal phone.

"Sprocket?" he barked.

"Yes, sir, it's me," said a high voice.

"Of course it's you, you idiot," said Curzon. Sprocket was in fact "the team" about which he had boasted to Donald Fenton. "Now listen. We've got a missing boy case. I want a hundred flyers and a photo in the usual dailies. There's a twenty-thousand-pound reward for news of the boy. Fiona'll bring everything down."

"Yes, sir. I'll see to it straightaway."

Milton Sprocket was a thin, pale young man who was never allowed upstairs because he had a local accent and had not been to the right school. MMM had the use of a basement room and a garage and it was there that he was to be found.

He was a man who took his work very seriously. After rather a sad childhood being bullied at school and failing his exams, Sprocket had taken a correspondence course at the College of Surveillance and Technology and got a Diploma in Detection and Tracking (or DDT for short). It was a first-class diploma because the college didn't give out any seconds or thirds, and after this his life had changed.

Sprocket was hardworking and neat. In his cubbyhole in the basement was a cabinet with a number of drawers, all carefully labeled, in which he kept his disguises. There was a drawer labeled: *mustaches, eyebrows, nose hair*. Another said *scabs, wounds, pimples, and boils*, and another read *spectacles, monocles, ear trumpets*. There was a wig stand in a corner, and a compartment for false teeth, and in a locked cabinet on the other wall lived a row of bottles labeled *spit, blood, pus,* and *phlegm*, which had been a special offer on the Internet.

But though being in disguise and stalking people was what Sprocket liked best, most of the room was given over to the latest technology. The gadgets upstairs were only for show; it was down here in the basement that the real stuff was to be found. There were fiber-optic cables for looking around corners, and underwater cameras with fins, and sat navs that told you where you were going and where you had been, and binoculars with night vision, and ultra-violet heat-sensing devices . . . and because some of these things were not very easy to understand, Sprocket had a tall pile of instruction manuals over which he pored for long hours, trying to work out exactly what went where.

Not only that, but Sprocket was also a poet. In the MMM garage next to his room was a white van that he used when he was detecting, and on the side of the van was a verse he had written quite by himself.

Have you lost it or misplaced it?

In a jiffy we will trace it!

The poem was written on a board that could slide out and be replaced by others if he was on a secret mission and both he and the van needed to be in dis-guise. For example, there was one for when he wanted to pretend to be a greengrocer, which went:

When your appetite's on edge,

We will bring you fruit and veg.

He was also working on a completely new verse that he meant to use when pretending to be a plumber, but it was giving him trouble. A poem like that had to be strong and powerful, but of course none of the words in it could actually be rude.

He pressed the repeat button on his phone and listened to a new message from Curzon.

"This is a big one, Sprocket. Go to it! No hanging about."

Sprocket smiled and rubbed his hands. He was just in the mood for an important and tricky case.

14

Nini

Greystoke House was a big stone building on the outskirts of Todcaster. From the street it looked forbidding and grim, but inside, the walls had been painted in bright colors. There was a nursery full of toys, and a room where the older children watched TV. Mrs. Platt, the housemother who was in charge, was a fat and friendly lady who did her best to be motherly. All the same, to the children who lived there, waiting to be placed with foster parents, it was still "The Home," a place in which no one wanted to stay longer than they needed.

The small girl who sat up in bed on the morning that the circus opened in Todcaster had no interest in being fostered. She seemed to have no interest in anything. She was a beautiful child with huge dark eyes, thick jet-black hair, and golden skin, but she lived in a closed world that nobody could reach.

She had come from an Indonesian island, a place of great beauty with lush forests, crystal rivers, and mountains shaped like big green cones, but a place, too, of sudden earthquakes and terrifying landslides. Nini's family had died in one of these, and she had been taken to an orphanage to be cared for by nuns.

It was a peaceful place set in the grounds of a temple where the monks prayed and chanted, and the little dogs that guarded them sat on the stone steps, keeping evil spirits at bay.

Then one day a rich businessman and his wife had come to the island for a holiday, seen the little girl playing quietly under a jacaranda tree, and decided to adopt her and bring her back to England.

For the first few months that Nini was with them, they were delighted with their pretty daughter and dressed her beautifully and showed her off to their friends. But then they found that the little girl did not learn to speak English as quickly as they hoped — in fact she did not speak at all. They took her to a doctor and another and another and were given a lot of names for what might be the matter with Nini, but no one could tell them what to do. She was not deaf, and she could see perfectly well, but she was enclosed in a world of her own.

Then one day when she had spent the whole day being tested in a hospital, Nini had a terrifying tantrum.

"They do that in the East," a friend had said. "It's called running amok."

This was too much for the couple, who had wanted a pretty, prattling doll, and they took her to the Children's Welfare Center and said they couldn't keep her. Since then, she had been in Greystoke House, not misbehaving, not being difficult, just not really being there at all.

Now she got out of bed and ran along the corridor, moving as lightly as a little ghost, and into the room where the older boys slept, and pulled at the duvet on the bed nearest the door.

Mick woke, saw who it was, and sat up.

"Today's the circus, Nini. We're going to the circus," he repeated.

He was a tough boy with ginger hair, freckles, and a cheerful open face. His grandfather had been a coal miner till the closure of the pits. For some reason Mick had become Nini's protector and the only person of whom she took any notice. "It'll be good," he went on. "There'll be horses and acrobats and clowns."

But Nini did not answer, only looked at him. He might have been telling her about a visit to the dentist. Mick sighed and reached for his clothes.

Greystoke House was not far from the common where the circus was encamped. The children walked there, shepherded by plump Mrs. Platt and a nursery assistant called Doreen. They danced along, excited by the treat to come. Only Nini, clutching Mick's hand, walked along in silence.

The circus was gearing up for the start. On a platform outside the big top, a small man with a mustache was juggling a mass of colored balls. Another man in spangled tights was beating a big drum.

"Come and see Henry's Circus, the eighth wonder of the world!" he shouted.

The Greystoke children were early. They filed into the front row. Mick sat down next to a boy of about his own age, with a white dog on his knee. Nini was beside him. Her legs, too short to reach the ground, stuck out in front of her.

"It's going to start," Mick told her.

But nothing moved in the beautiful, masklike face.

Hal, holding on to Fleck, was sick with nerves. In half an hour the Dog Family Murgatroyd would do their turn, and if it went wrong they would be banished from the circus. All the same, he turned to smile at the boy who had just come in with a group of children and was sitting next to him. He had ginger hair and looked friendly.

The houselights dimmed, the band struck up. Mr. Henry, in his ringmaster's clothes, cracked his whip.

The procession came first. The horses, the clowns, the tumblers and acrobats, Pauline's Parrots all sitting on her shoulders. There was a burst of clapping — and the show began.

The Texas Terrors galloped in first — a string of horses ridden bareback by three men who leapt from one gleaming back to the other. . . . The Dainty Danielas — a group of girls in shining costumes who climbed on one another's shoulders and threw one another up in the air . . . The Comedy Horse, a pony who followed his master around the ring trying to get sugar lumps out of his pockets . . . A stupendous display on the high wire with men and women pretending to push one another off . . .

Hal was holding his breath. The time had come. Fleck whined once and Hal shushed him.

"And now, Elsa's Fabulous Dogs in The Murgatroyd Family Go to Their Wedding," announced the ringmaster.

The clowns came on first. They wheeled in a huge bath filled with water, and carried buckets and a ladder. They were trying to get ready for the wedding feast, but everything kept going wrong. The legs came off the table they were scrubbing; the balloons they were trying to blow up burst in their faces or floated out of reach; one of the clowns fell backward into the bath. . . .

A tent with a big notice on it saying *The Church* had been put up near the entrance, and Rupert appeared and sat in front of it in his bow tie and silk waistcoat. Another lot of clowns came in on stilts, carrying trays of wobbling jellies and colored streamers in which they got entangled, and they threshed about and pretended to cry.

And now, to a fanfare from the band, the cart pulled by Otto made its entry.

Otto was wretchedly nervous but Francine had given him a good talking-to and he managed to trot steadily three-quarters of the way around the ring. Li-Chee in his little bonnet and Honey in her frilly hat sat in their seats, but Francine was standing up on her hind legs. With her white wreath and the enthusiastic little yaps she gave, she was obviously an eager bride.

But now something happened that the children had not bargained for. The audience broke into a storm of clapping and as the sound grew louder, Otto began to tremble. He had faced all sorts of dangers in Switzerland, climbing up rock faces and plunging into dangerous crevasses to rescue trapped climbers, but this noise was horrible; it was not to be borne. His eyes rolled and he stopped dead.

And Li-Chee, who would have done anything for Otto, jumped down from the cart with his bonnet askew and reappeared beneath Otto's legs. He meant only to reassure his friend, but it looked as though he was trying to pull the cart, and everybody laughed. Not at the clowns now, but at the gallant little dog.

It was at this moment that Mick turned in amazement to the little girl beside him. Nini was leaning forward intently, her whole face alight, her eyes fixed in wonder at the Peke.

In the ring, no one, for a moment, knew what to do. Otto was standing stock-still, his head hanging. There was no way he was going to pull the cart as far as the church.

And once again it was Francine, that old trouper, who took over. She leapt from the cart, but she did not run toward her bridegroom. She charged in the other direction, making noises of terror. She had changed the plot and become a dog who did not want to be married, who wanted to be free — and Rupert caught on at once. He jumped to his feet and gave chase, barking angrily — a bridegroom who wasn't going to be done out of his bride.

The two poodles rolled over together, but Francine escaped and ran up a ladder and took a flying leap into the arms of one of the clowns. Rupert followed her. But now the clowns understood the game. They pretended to catch Francine; they grabbed her and lost her and hit their foreheads in despair. Around and around the ring went the fleeing bride, between the legs of the clowns, flying over the table, hiding behind the bath, yelping in mock terror — and around and around went Rupert, the thwarted bridegroom, following her trick for trick.

The slapstick grew wilder and wilder. The clowns stepped into the buckets, fell on the balloons and burst them . . . Li-Chee left Otto and joined in, yapping at the top of his voice.

Meanwhile, Fleck, on Hal's lap, had been getting more and more excited. All his friends were up there and he wanted desperately to be brave and join them, but he couldn't quite do it. Then, in a sudden burst of courage, he jumped off Hal's knee, leapt over the barrier — and landed in the bath of water. For a moment he paddled up and down, then he scrambled out, shook himself, and joined in the chase.

But now came Honey. She was, after all, the mother and she couldn't bear the mess and muddle any longer. She leapt from the cart, still in her frilly hat, and began trying to herd the clowns, the dogs, the balloons — everything she could see — toward the exit.

Around and around they went, Francine and Rupert in the lead, then Li-Chee, Fleck, and Otto with the cart. And around and around went the clowns.

But they still hadn't left the ring and Honey now called on all her old sheepdog skills. She turned and ran in the other direction to meet Francine, her runaway daughter, head-on. The music grew to a crescendo, everyone disappeared through the exit — and the lights went out.

And the audience roared and stamped and clapped and cheered, while behind the scenes, Mr. Henry and George looked at each other and grinned.

Performing dogs are valuable, but dog clowns are pure gold.

● ● ●

"Well, we did it," said Pippa triumphantly. "I reckon we can stay till Berwick and then it's hardly any distance to your grandparents'. Even if they do something quite different next time, Mr. Henry won't send us away."

They had taken the dogs back to the truck and were helping out in the tent where the performing animals were housed. For a small sum the audience could visit them in their cages after the show.

"Excuse me." Hal turned to find the ginger-haired boy who'd been sitting next to him.

Clutching his hand was the tiny girl with jet-black hair. "I was wondering if there was any chance of seeing the little dog that tried to pull the cart. The Peke. She's nutty about him."

Nini looked up. "Small dog," she said.

"I think she's seen dogs like that where she came from. Temple dogs they were, guarding the monks and chasing away evil spirits and all that stuff. But it's amazing because she's never taken notice of anything up till now. I've got permission from our housemother, as long as we're not too long. She's taken the others to look at the liberty horses."

"Small dog," repeated Nini, who never spoke.

"He's in the truck with the others — just across the grass," said Hal. "Come on, we'll show you."

They were greeted by a chorus of friendly barks. Mick lifted Nini up onto the hay bales and she disappeared into the huddle of dogs. When they looked at her again, they saw something unexpected. Nini had not picked up Li-Chee or hugged him. She was sitting cross-legged in front of him, not touching him, murmuring to him in her own language while Li-Chee stood very still, his face lifted respectfully up to hers. It was obvious that he understood every word.

"You can't imagine what a thing this is," said Mick, and in a few words he gave them Nini's history.

The children had moved a little way away, giving Nini as long as they could. They were talking quietly, beginning to make friends, when two stable hands came past.

"Look at this," said one. "Here on page two." There was a rustle of pages being turned. "That's the spit an' image of the boy with the white dog. The one that's staying with Bill and Myra. Don't tell me it isn't."

The children, hidden by the side of the truck, froze into silence.

The other stable hand whistled through his teeth. "'Twenty-thousand-pound reward for news of him,' it says. It can't be the same boy."

"Maybe not. But it looks like him and it's worth a chance. The phone number's here."

The men moved away out of earshot. Mick, looking at Hal and Pippa, saw the shock on their faces.

"I don't want to pry, but if there's anything I can do to help?" he said. "I mean if you're on the run or something." And as the children exchanged glances, he said, "You don't have to explain, I'll help you just the same. It makes no difference to me."

Hal only hesitated for a moment. The redheaded boy was probably quite as much in need of twenty thousand pounds as the circus lads. But Hal felt certain that Mick was to be trusted, that he was honest and truthful and brave. He said, "Yes, maybe you could help. We'll have to leave here at once, but we don't really know where we are or anything. We ought to hide somewhere overnight, I suppose, and then start off at dawn."

Pippa looked at him, frowning. It was usually she who made the decisions — and they knew nothing about the boy.

"You can spend the night at our place," said Mick. "There's a big boiler room in the basement. No one goes there. I know where the key is. I'll get it and get some food down there and blankets. There's only Mrs. Platt at night and she sleeps like a log."

"Would you really?" said Hal. "I think that might work. But how do we get to you? Did you come in a bus?"

Mick shook his head.

"We walked. It's only twenty minutes from here. I'll draw you a map."

"What about the other children?" asked Pippa. "Can you trust them not to give us away?"

Mick said, "Yes."

They left a note for George. It was hard lying to someone who had been so helpful, but there was nothing else to do. The note said that Aunt Elsa had gotten in touch and told them that she couldn't manage to get north because her brother-in-law was in the hospital, so they were taking the overnight bus back to London. Fortunately Bill and Myra had gone out to the cinema, so the children were able to say good-bye by letter, and to thank them for all they had done.

Then they gathered up their belongings and went to fetch the dogs.

At first all went well. The dogs liked the idea of a late-night walk. They noticed that Pippa had strapped on her knapsack and Hal carried his bag, and both of them wore their hoodies. For Fleck and Otto and Li-Chee and Honey this meant that they were off on another adventure and they were ready for it.

But not Francine. Francine knew that they were leaving. Leaving the circus — and leaving Rupert.

She sat down where she was. She threw back her head and she howled. It was the most desperate and forlorn sound the children had ever heard. And from George's camper where he now slept, Rupert replied and came to her.

What followed was almost unbearable. The poodles stood together in the dusk, their bodies so close that they might have been one thing. They did not bark or complain; they only shivered as sorrow gripped them.

Hal and Pippa watched, and the other dogs, too. Could they force Francine away? She loved the life of the circus, and she loved Rupert. It was a proper enduring passion, they knew that.

Yet could they go on without her? This flight was an adventure they all shared.

The two poodles still stood like statues. No one else existed for them. Otto took a few steps toward them and then stopped. He and Francine had been friends for a long time, but he did nothing. Francine would have to decide this for herself.

"Come on, Hal," said Pippa, who could bear it no longer. "We have to get on. She's got a right to stay."

They turned and made their way slowly over the trampled grass. They had reached the entrance to the circus when Francine gave a last, heartrending howl. Then she turned away from Rupert and raced after them.

15

Greystoke House

Mrs. Platt was snoring — a great juddering noise that sounded as though it would rattle the window frames. One of the boys whom Mick had put on guard leaned out of the landing window and signaled to Mick in the shrubbery to say that all was clear.

In the girls' room, Nini lay silently in her bed, but she was not asleep.

It was almost dark now. They would be here soon — and Mick settled down to wait.

The dogs walked slowly. They had had a hard day and their performance in the ring had tired them. The last dog, as they made their way through the unfamiliar streets, was Francine. She was usually so light on her feet, but now she could hardly put one paw in front of the other, and her head was down. Every step was taking her farther from where she wanted to be and she looked as though she didn't care whether she lived or died.

Hal was trying to read Mick's map, hastily scribbled on the back of an envelope. In the failing light they took a wrong turn — but at last they came to the iron gate of Greystoke House.

There was no time to be anxious — Mick was there in a moment.

"You must be absolutely quiet," Pippa told the dogs. They understood, and followed as Mick led them around to the back of the building and down a short flight of stone steps.

They found themselves in a boiler room with a bare stone floor, coiled pipes around the walls, a big heater humming in one corner. The windows were shuttered and a faint blue light hung overhead. It was dry and warm, and in a corner they found blankets and pillows that Mick's friends had "borrowed" from the storeroom and brought down in secret. A big bowl of water, and plates piled with meatballs and rice, pinched from the children's supper, were laid out on the floor.

"Did you have to go without your meal to give us this?" asked Pippa.

Mick shrugged. "The girl who serves supper is pretty sloppy. It isn't difficult to get stuff off the table, and we don't go hungry here. The food's dull, but it's perfectly OK." Then he said, "Nothing happens, that's the worst of living in a place like this. We'd do worse things than going without meatballs to know we can help."

The dogs were too well trained to start eating without permission, but they looked hungrily at the plates, and then at Hal and Pippa, and when they got the signal to begin, they put their heads down and ate.

All except Francine. Francine looked at the food and turned her head away and walked to a quiet corner of the room, wanting only to be alone with her grief.

"Come along, Francine," said Pippa, fondling her head. "Try just a little."

But Francine wouldn't eat. She gave her paw to

Pippa a few times to say she understood that Pippa was sorry for her. Pippa wasn't to worry, she was saying, but right now she couldn't swallow even the smallest mouthful.

"We'll be keeping watch," said Mick. "Someone will wake you first thing in the morning so that you can be off in case the boiler man comes — though he's not due tomorrow."

Hal and Pippa looked at him. There was nothing to say except thank you, so they said it, and several times over.

"We won't forget this," said Hal. "Not ever. And if there's anything we can do for you, well, you know..."

Now that they were temporarily safe, Hal and Pippa had time to wonder what the stable hand would do, and how likely they were to be pursued. It was not so far to Hal's grandfather overland, but it couldn't be done in less than two days' hard walking, across moorland and fields, toward the coast.

But soon they stopped whispering and curled up on the blanket, and although the stone floor was not exactly comfortable, they slept.

The dogs slept, too. Otto lay close to Francine and his reassuring bulk did something to calm her. Once or twice she woke up briefly and whined, remembering what she had lost, but then Otto would move closer to her, and she was quiet again. Fleck lay across Hal's feet, his facecloth beside him.

Upstairs, Mrs. Platt still snored, the breath wheezing in and out of her great bulk, and while they heard the steady, unpleasant noise she made, Mick and his friends knew that the fugitives were safe.

But in the room she shared with the other little girls, Nini sat up in bed. She had been waiting, and now she pushed back the bedspread and fetched the brush and comb from her locker and crept, silent as a wraith, along the corridor.

At the top of the stairs she ran into Mick, who was keeping watch.

"See small dog," she said. "See Li-Chee."

Mick stared at her. How did she know? Had she overheard something when he was talking to Hal and Pippa or did she have some other way of knowing things? Whatever it was, he couldn't take any risks.

Even Mrs. Platt couldn't sleep through one of Nini's tantrums.

He took her hand. "You can see Li-Chee, but you must be very, very quiet or they will take him away. Do you understand? Absolutely silent."

Nini nodded, and he led her down the cellar steps to the door of the boiler room.

The little girl knew about moving silently. She opened the door of the cellar so quietly that the huddle of dogs hardly stirred and the children did not wake. Only Li-Chee, who was on the edge of the circle because he had given his place beside Otto to Francine, raised his head.

He was surprised to be woken and at first he wondered if it wasn't one of the other dogs she wanted because he was used to being small and unimportant and only suitable for old ladies. But as Nini knelt down in front of him he realized that it was really him she wanted, just as it had been him in the truck, and though he was very sleepy and would have liked to close his eyes again, he made himself stay awake and began to lick her wrist.

Once again, Nini did not hug him or try and pick him up. Instead, she took up her brush and comb and very slowly, very carefully, she groomed the long, silky golden coat and smoothed back the hair that had tumbled into his eyes.

And as she brushed and combed and tidied him, she was back in her homeland, helping the girls who danced in the temple to prepare the little guard dogs that they worshipped for the festivals.

Everything came back to her — everything she missed so terribly that she had shut it out completely: the scent of jasmine, the temple bells, the quiet voices of the nuns in the orphanage . . . the warmth, the sun on her skin . . . and her own language.

Steadily, quietly, Nini brushed and combed and murmured. And as she worked, the homesickness that had crippled her and turned her into a mute came out, and the tears she had not been able to shed ran down her cheeks.

And Li-Chee stood trustingly in front of her. Already he loved her. She had chosen him and he had chosen her, but as the grooming went on, there came from his throat a low rumbling . . . a kind of gargling sound — and Nini put down her brush. She recognized the noise Li-Chee was making. In his polite way he was telling her that he did not want to be groomed. He did not want to be worshipped.

He wanted to be understood. To go forward . . .

For a moment Nini sat still, thinking. Then she gave a small shake of her head, and let it all go out of her — her memories, her sadness. She looked around the dimly lit room at the other dogs. She thought of the very small girl in the nursery who had tugged at her skirts, wanting to be her friend. She thought of the games they played in the garden of Greystoke House, the squirrel they had tamed, the cartoons they watched at bedtime. She thought of Mick.

It was time to move on.

"Wait here," she said to Li-Chee.

She crept out again and made her way to Mrs. Platt's sitting room. The scissors were where she remembered, at the bottom of the sewing basket. Nini took them, being careful to carry them with the points down as she had been taught, and made her way downstairs again. It would not be easy, but she would do it. She would be brave.

Li-Chee was waiting where she had left him.

"I won't hurt you," she said. "Just stand still."

Then she began to cut, and to snip and to cut again, and as she did so, the golden silky coat that had imprisoned Li-Chee fell silently to the floor.

Pippa was the first to wake, and it was all she could do not to let out a cry of horror.

"What have you done?" she said. "For heaven's sake — oh, the poor, poor dog!"

Nini did not answer; she only smiled.

"He's ruined," said Pippa. "He'll never be in a show again. Nobody will want a dog like that."

But now Li-Chee got to his feet and shook himself, making sure that it had really happened. And then he went crazy. He raced around the cellar, he rolled over and over waving his paws in the air, he let out high-pitched yelps of sheer delight.

He could see, he could move, he was revealed as the dog he really was. A lion dog, a fighter, the guardian of emperors, not a pampered plaything for old ladies. His little squashed face looked out at the clear, clean world, and his pop eyes glowed in the morning light. Someone had understood him; someone had found out who he really was!

Hal woke then and saw what had happened, but before he could say anything Mick came in and said it was time to go.

16

Sprocket Gets a Call

The stable hand lost very little time. As soon as the horses were bedded down for the night, he made his call.

Curzon, of course, was no longer in his office. He often did not return after a long lunch, and Fiona never stayed once he had gone. So it was in Sprocket's little cubbyhole that the phone rang, and he seized it eagerly.

"MMM here. Milton Sprocket speaking."

He listened, getting more and more excited, trying to take notes with one hand.

"I'm pretty sure it's him," the voice at the other

end was saying. "Looks just like the photo. You did say twenty thousand pounds? No funny business?"

"Yes, yes," said Sprocket eagerly. "Now just tell me exactly where you are. Give me your coordinates."

But the stable hand had not heard of coordinates.

"Don't know what they are, mate. We're in Todcaster with Henry's Circus. And you better get up here quickly because we'll be on the move again soon."

When he put the receiver down, Sprocket was in a state of feverish agitation. It was clear that he had to act straightaway and not wait for Curzon's instructions. What's more, it seemed that the boy had not been kidnapped as everyone thought, but had run away. Children did run away to join the circus, Sprocket knew, and that meant he would not want to be recaptured and taken home. And this, in turn, meant some serious disguises while the boy was being stalked and cornered and brought back. The van would have to be disguised, too — probably best to put on the greengrocer poem. They'd like the idea of fresh vegetables up in the north.

Sprocket hurried to the cabinet and opened the top drawer. He was a fair man and tried hard not to have any favorites among his mustaches, but there was one that he did love particularly. It was a rich nut brown color and wonderfully bushy, and it settled against his upper lip like the softest fur. He put it on and immediately felt ready for a great adventure. Then he packed up a couple of wigs, an ear trumpet, and some pimples and boils, but not the scars — you couldn't have everything. At the last minute he added the bottle of blood but left the one labeled *saliva* — there would be places up there where one could spit if necessary.

Running backward and forward, Sprocket loaded the van, putting in the new sat nav, the infrared heat-sensing device, the binoculars with night vision. . . . The little packet containing Hal's toothbrush and his handkerchiefs went in the secret compartment behind the driving seat. And of course he had a case ready packed with pajamas and a change of underclothes. Sprocket's mother had always been careful to see that her son understood the importance of being fresh and clean not just on top but all the way through.

He was removing the board that said *Have you lost*

it or misplaced it? In a jiffy we will trace it! and sliding in the one that said *When your appetite's on edge, We will bring you fruit and veg,* when he remembered that he had not left a message for Curzon. So he went back into the cubbyhole and sent a coded message from his computer to Curzon's computer upstairs, telling him where he had gone.

Then he eased the van out of the garage and set off for the highway. As he passed a row of shops he saw a big notice in one of the windows in which a light still burned.

Easy Pets, it said. *Pedigree Dogs to Rent.*

Sprocket drove on without a second glance. He was not fond of dogs.

The light should not have been burning at Easy Pets so late. Kayley had been due home an hour ago. She still had the flu and should have been in bed. But one of the dogs, the mastiff who had eaten her mistress's finger by mistake, was running a temperature. Her nose was dry and she was off her food and Kayley sat with her, wondering whether to call out the vet so late. The Carkers never came to the dogs after hours.

She was feeling wretched. She went on missing the dogs in Room A more than she would have thought possible, and she was terribly worried about Pippa. The police had been back asking a lot more questions and she felt that it was only a matter of time before they found out that it was Pippa who had been in the building on Sunday night.

She was putting on her coat when Queen Tilly started up again. The Mexican hairless was disgusted. She was a dog who in a way was born disgusted, but since her roommates had disappeared, life at Easy Pets had become impossible. The five dogs who had replaced Otto and Francine and the others were simply not fit to associate with a Mexican hairless who had belonged to an heiress and eaten off silver plates. There was an Airedale who suffered from hair balls, a dachshund who drooled, and some others that it was better not to think about. So she twitched and screeched and yelped and grumbled, till Kayley came to her in the compound and put another cushion in her padded sleeping basket and gave her a drink of milk.

When she got home at last, Kayley was so very exhausted she could hardly put one foot in front of the other. But one of the twins was stuck with his homework and needed help, and Grandfather had to be wheeled out to the corner store. Nothing could convince him that he wasn't going to buy back the family farm with his winning lottery ticket.

Mrs. O'Brian was still out, working late for Mrs. Naryan. For a moment Kayley wondered whether to go and fetch her. The Naryans were always so friendly and welcoming, and the warm house with its wonderful silks and perfumes seemed very tempting on this miserable night. Once when it was raining badly, Mrs. Naryan had sent her mother home in her husband's silver Rolls-Royce, a car so silent and so beautiful that it was hard to believe that it was just an ordinary machine and not something out of a dream.

But she was too tired to go anywhere. When she had finished her chores, Kayley picked up the phone meaning to ring Pippa — she had an emergency number for the school camp and perhaps it was best to warn her. But then she thought better of it. It seemed cruel to spoil Pippa's holiday, and she put the phone down again and climbed wearily into her bed, and tried to sleep.

•   •   •

At MMM the phone rang, and rang, and rang again as Donald tried desperately to get news of his son, while upstairs, Albina, wearing no makeup for the first time in her adult life, wept over the beige carpet that had arrived that afternoon to replace the blue one in Hal's room.

17

Honey on the Hill

Mick had told them the quickest way out of Todcaster. They had walked steadily along quiet streets, which turned into country lanes as they came closer to the moors. Li-Chee had started off very full of himself. He had been a small dog before, but now, shorn of his golden pelt, he was a very small dog indeed, not much bigger than a well-fed rat. Inside, though, he was a lion, and when Pippa tried to carry him part of the way, he yelped with outrage. But after a few hours everybody needed a rest. Now they were leaning against a low stone wall, and around them were fields and low hills. A curlew called, a soft wind blew. Mick had managed to find some bread and butter for them and a few cookies, which they shared with the dogs.

"I don't know why he did all this for us," said Hal. "I hope I get a chance to repay him someday."

"You could do it by going on being his friend," said Pippa — and Hal looked at her, surprised. He hadn't been brought up to think that friendship was enough. You had to give people something solid: a present or money. But of course Pippa was right.

They were thinking of moving on when they heard a piercing whistle from the hill behind them. The dogs pricked up their ears, as they did at any sound, and flopped down again.

Except for Honey. One minute Honey was beside them. The next second she had jumped the wall — and was gone.

Old Selby the shepherd had come out of his cottage in a gloomy mood. His back ached, his knees were stiff, but that wasn't what was making him feel wretched. His niece had found a place where he could spend the rest of his life in comfort: a room in a block of apartments called Rosewood, built as sheltered housing in the town. Rooms like that were hard to find and she had showed him around proudly.

"See how warm it is," she said, pointing to the radiators. "And there's a warden here all the time. If you want anything, you just have to press the bell."

It was very kind of his niece, but when he thought of Rosewood his blood ran cold. He had not found it warm but unbearably stuffy. The people looking out of their rooms to give him a friendly greeting as he went down the corridor made him feel stifled, and out of the window you could see nothing but houses and still more houses.

Selby had been a shepherd on these hills for fifty years. He'd lived in the same stone cottage, run the same breed of sheep, woken each day to the sound of birdsong and the soughing of the wind. But old age had overtaken him, as it had overtaken his dog, Billy. Billy had been one of the best sheepdogs in the country, but now he limped and wheezed when he had to run fast.

Well, it was no good fighting against what had to be. His niece was right. He couldn't really manage any longer. He'd have to sell the flock and find a home for

Billy, and with luck both he and the dog wouldn't last too long.

Meanwhile, the sheep had to be gathered from the hill and brought down into the fold for dipping. The dog had done it a thousand times, and now he waited, ready for the command. He would go on till his lungs burst, but Selby knew how much it cost him.

Selby fetched his crook and sent him off. Billy ran up to the flock and lay down behind the sheep. He was panting pathetically, but he waited, ready as always to do his job.

Old Selby put his fingers to his mouth and whistled, the sign that Billy was to start the gathering. The sheep were widely scattered today, and as obstinate as only sheep can be, and they knew that Billy was no longer the threat he had once been. He began to round them up, but a couple of ewes broke away and went off to the left. The dog chivvied them back, but now the rest of the flock was separating again. One old ewe, a thoroughly bad-tempered animal, had begun to graze.

Old Selby, watching, shook his head. It was no good hoping. He was too old to train another dog. There was no escaping Rosewood.

But now, when Selby was feeling so wretched, there was worse to come. A honey-colored blur streaked up the hill and headed straight for the flock. A fox? No, a stray dog. A sheep worrier as likely as not.

"Blasted townies, letting their dogs off the leash," he grumbled.

He began to struggle up the hill, waving his stick, knowing there was nothing he could do if the dog was a killer.

Then he stopped dead and stared.

The new dog had come around behind the unruly flock in a wide run and now, head low, totally concentrating — sometimes darting left or right to check breakaways — she was gathering the animals into a tight bunch. Then she dropped down behind them, ears pricked, with Billy at her side.

She was waiting for instructions. A trained dog? Was it possible?

Half wondering if he was dreaming, Selby whistled again, giving the signal to start the fetch.

And slowly, expertly, the unknown dog began to move the flock down the hill toward the fold. Any stragglers were immediately brought back. She seemed to know what the sheep were going to do before they knew it themselves. She could run like the wind when it was needful, but there was no hassling, no snapping at their heels. With Billy helping as best he could, she sent them steadily to where they needed to be.

For Honey, as she worked, the miserable months she had spent at Easy Pets fell away. It all came back to her — how to anticipate the movements of the flock, how to prevent trouble. . . . She could feel the wind blowing through her coat. Her eyes shone. She could have run like this forever.

Within minutes the sheep were streaming like a white river into the fold, and Selby moved forward to close the gate.

"That'll do," he said to both the dogs, and Honey, who had flopped down beside him, looked up, her plumed tail waving, for she remembered those words from her former life, and knew what they meant. That the job was over, and had been done well.

Ten minutes later Selby sat in his kitchen, drinking a cup of tea. Honey was lying on the hearth rug beside Billy, who had made room for her, and as he looked at her, Old Selby allowed himself to dream.

What if it really was a miracle? What if this wonder dog had come to save him and his flock? With a dog like that he could last another five years, and then they'd know what they could do with Rosewood.

He was interrupted by a knock at the door and he opened it to find a small girl, breathless and looking very worried.

"I'm sorry to bother you but you haven't seen a dog — a rough collie, white and black and sable? She just took off and vanished when she heard a whistle."

Selby let her in and pointed to the rug.

"I thought it was too good to be true," he said as Honey got to her feet, tail wagging, and came to greet Pippa. "You know she's a proper sheepdog, don't you? One of the best. You should have seen her on the hill."

"Yes, I know. She was trained somewhere not far from here, but the man who owned her had to sell his farm. She was bought by a family with small children who teased her and —"

Pippa broke off. She had nearly been stupid enough to mention Easy Pets.

Honey was still welcoming Pippa, rubbing her nose against Pippa's legs. It was Pippa who had set her free. She remembered the other dogs, she remembered the journey they were taking.

But then she ran back to Selby and looked up at him. Here was her true master; it was here that she could do her real work and be herself. And she sat down between Selby and Pippa, in a moment of confusion and despair.

Old Selby bent down and pulled her ears. He knew he could keep her. If he said "sit" she would sit. If he said "stay" she would stay, and she would do this till the day she died.

Pippa was silent, remembering Francine. Honey would have to choose, but was it fair to make her? She was a different kind of dog. There had been a girl in Pippa's class whose parents had decided to get divorced. The girl had managed all right till she was asked to choose which of her parents she wanted to live with, and after that she had simply fallen apart.

If it was so hard for a person to decide, could one ask it of a dog?

In the end it was old Selby who did the choosing. He had never taken another person's dog, and he would not do so now, but the next moments were the hardest he could remember.

He raised his stick and spoke to Honey.

"Go on. Be off with you," he said in his gruffest voice. "Get out of here."

Honey whined and looked up at him and licked his hand, but his stick was still raised, and slowly, very slowly, looking back over her shoulder, she followed Pippa out of the door.

Selby stood on his porch and watched them go. Miracles occurred all right, but not, it seemed, for him. His eyes were watering, and angrily he wiped them with his sleeve.

"Blasted wind," he muttered.

Then he turned back into the house and went to phone his niece.

18

The Dumper

Kevin Dawks was a kind man. One knew this because he was always helping people. He helped the manager of the supermarket in the town with the pile of rotting vegetables and plastic bags and oozing paint tins that wouldn't go in the Dumpsters, and he helped the owner of the pub with the old TV and the bicycle his son had written off — and he helped the man in the garage with the oilcans and bottles of poisonous liquids that were cluttering up his shelves.

He helped them by taking these things away and finding a place for them. The places he found were some way out of towns and villages, in a quiet part of the countryside. It might be in a bluebell wood or a river valley or a freshly planted field. Kevin didn't mind, as long as it wasn't overlooked by anyone and he could tip out his load of filth without anybody seeing.

Of course, he charged quite a lot for this service. Being a dumper is a dangerous business, and he always had to look out for the police or busybodies who said that what he was doing was illegal and disgusting. And because he didn't make as much money as he deserved to, he had other jobs. He stored things that had fallen off the backs of trucks, like cartons of cigarettes and bits of jewelry, or tools that had been nicked and needed to be hid before being sold on — and he kept these in a lockup shed on the edge of the moor.

The children had kept up a steady pace after they left the shepherd, and by early afternoon they were on a quiet country road leading up to the moors. Beside them, in a dip sheltered by birch trees, ran a crystal stream.

"My grandfather says you can drink from all the streams up here. The water comes off the Cheviots and it's the cleanest in the country," said Hal. "If you go on ahead, I'll just go down and fill my water bottle."

"All right, but don't be long," said Pippa.

She went on with the other dogs while Fleck and Hal scrambled down the steep sides of the little valley. It was a beautiful place. The bracken fronds were uncurling, bluebells flowered between the birches . . . they were magical, these sheltered dells.

Fleck had been running ahead, but now he came back to Hal and stopped in front of him, holding up a front paw.

"What's the matter, Fleck?"

Fleck whimpered, and Hal saw a piece of rusty wire caught between his toes. Hal took it out, and it was then he noticed the smell.

It was a smell that seemed completely unreal in this lovely place. A vile, sick-making stench of decay and rottenness.

Then he saw it: a pile of garbage spilling down to the edge of the water. There was a torn mattress; half-open tins of oil oozed onto the grass. A heap of rotting food burst out of a plastic bag, and an old sofa lay on its side, its rusty springs sticking up from the stained upholstery. Some of the refuse had been tipped into the stream itself; fetid bubbles of gas broke the surface of the water. A twisted electric heater was wedged against a boulder. A young birch sapling had fallen across the stream, broken by the weight of an iron bath.

And over everything, this unspeakable smell . . .

Hal hardly remembered how he got back up the bank. He was in a state of shock. Who could do this; who could turn this wonderful place into a garbage heap? He was still getting his breath, tying up his shoelace at the edge of the road, when a pickup drove past him, braked, and backed toward him.

Kevin had just finished dumping his load by the stream before Hal came, and had had a rest, dozing in his truck, as people do when they have done a good morning's work. He was setting off again, bound for his lockup on the moor, when he saw a boy sitting on the side of the road. The boy had fair hair and was wearing a blue hoodie — and for some reason he seemed familiar.

The hair began to rise on the back of Kevin's neck. He braked and reached for the newspaper.

Yes, it was what he'd thought. He'd seen the ad when he was having his breakfast and now he peered at it again. This was the boy for whom they were offering twenty thousand pounds' reward! He peered again, but there was no mistaking it. Hardly able to believe his luck, he leaned out of the window of the cab, and in his oiliest voice, he said:

"Want a lift?"

Hal shook his head.

"Thanks, but I'm with a friend. I'm just going to catch up with her."

Kevin grinned. The boy was obviously lying. There'd been no mention of a friend in the ad, but he'd go along with it.

"Well, I'm going that way. I'll pick her up and give both of you a lift to the village. It's not far. My name's Kevin, by the way."

Hal hesitated. But it was true he'd been longer than he intended. He'd trusted Mick and it had been all right. People in the north were known to be friendly.

"All right," he said. "Thanks."

He climbed into the cab and pulled Fleck in after him, but Fleck was behaving badly. As the engine revved up again he began to growl and show his teeth.

"Quiet, Fleck," said Hal.

But Fleck, usually so obedient, took no notice. Hal was looking down, trying to soothe him, and at first he did not notice that the van had swerved sharply to the left, up a rutted track.

"Stop," he said. "That's not the way. We should be going straight on," and as Kevin took no notice, he said loudly, "Where are you going?"

"You'll see soon enough," said Kevin. His voice was quite different now, harsh and ugly.

They drove uphill toward an isolated shed. But Fleck was going crazy. He jumped off Hal's lap and tried to clamber on the steering wheel, all the time barking at the top of his voice.

"Shut up, you little tyke," said Kevin. And he seized the dog by the scruff of his neck and threw him out of the window.

Hal screamed and tried to get out, too, but

Kevin put out one arm and held him in a grip of steel. He wasn't going to let twenty thousand pounds get away.

While Fleck yowled in anguish on the path, the pickup drove up to a stone hut with a corrugated iron roof, standing by itself on the edge of the moor. Pulling the struggling Hal out, Kevin dragged him to the door and pushed him in.

"Fleck!" screamed Hal.

Then the door was slammed shut, the bolts pushed across, and it was padlocked.

Kevin walked away, thoroughly pleased with himself. Now for a phone call to the number in the advertisement and then — twenty thousand pounds!

The wretched dog was still yowling and whining, trying to get to Hal in the shed. Kevin picked up a stone and threw it hard, and it hit the cur on the side. Then he took his cell phone out of his pocket and went a little way up the hill to get a signal.

Fleck was absolutely beside himself, trying to reach Hal. The stone hadn't drawn blood but it had bruised his shoulder. He could hear Hal's voice inside, frantically shouting his name.

For a few minutes Fleck ran uselessly around and around the hut, trying to find a way in. Then quite suddenly, he took off and raced like the wind down the hill and along the road.

Pippa was getting annoyed. What on earth was Hal doing? It shouldn't take so long to fill a water bottle. The dogs had been sitting around her obediently, waiting, but now they got to their feet and stared at the road, their noses twitching. Something was coming toward them — a white streak that, as they watched, turned into Fleck. But this was Fleck as no one had seen him. Not a wistful mongrel but a messenger bringing unspeakable news.

He raced up to the dogs, panting terribly, but he wouldn't rest. He jumped up at them, he shoved his nose into their sides, all the time talking in frantic barks.

"Where's Hal?" asked Pippa, her heart beginning to pound. "Where is he, Fleck?"

Fleck ran up to her, then back to the dogs. He started off up the road, looking back over his shoulder, but at first they did not follow. Then quite suddenly they understood, and a change came over these gentle domesticated pets. As one, they tore off up the track, with Fleck in the lead, and Pippa saw something that she was to remember all her life — the hunting pack, its blood up, closing in for the kill. Even Li-Chee, bouncing over the heather in the wake of the others, felt the blood of the gray wolf pounding in his veins. For wolves these dogs had been in the distant past, and wolves they had become again.

Kevin had made his phone call and, feeling very pleased with himself, he stretched out on the grass. The boy was still hammering on the door, but he'd get tired of it soon enough. There was nothing to do now except wait till he could hand him over.

And then, all the things he had promised himself — a new truck, the deposit on a little bungalow, a trip to Las Vegas. That snooty girl in the checkout would go out with him fast enough when he was loaded, thought Kevin, going off into a doze.

He woke to find two huge paws on his chest and an enormous pair of jaws, with a row of terrifying teeth, salivating into his face.

Then he felt both his legs being worried and bitten, his trousers ripped, as Francine took one leg and Honey the other.

"Stop!" screamed Kevin in agony. "Let go. Let go!"

And now Li-Chee, who had not been able to keep up with the others, came panting up, leapt onto Kevin's stomach, disappeared under Otto's chest, and fastened his needle-sharp teeth on Kevin's nose.

This was too much. Kevin struggled to his feet and in a welter of furious dogs, he staggered toward his van. Managing to shake off the Peke, blood pouring from his nose, he reached for the door handle.

But now it was Fleck's turn. Before Kevin could open the door, the Tottenham terrier raced up to him, sprang up — and bit him savagely in the behind.

And Kevin stumbled, fell forward onto the foot plate, and passed out.

It was there that Pippa found him, and after that everything went very quickly. Hal's thumps from inside the hut grew louder. Pippa ran up to the door and saw the padlock. Searching the lout's trousers, she found the key. Within minutes Hal was free and trying to calm his ecstatic dog, while Pippa relocked the door.

"We'll have to go up onto the moors," she said when she heard what had happened. "We can't risk the road now. While the sun's up we ought to be able to navigate all right. It's practically due east to the coast."

They set off up the hill, the dogs still excitedly circling them. The going was hard over the rough ground, but they did not dare to slow down till they were sure that Kevin was not following them. After a couple of hours the children were exhausted.

"I'm going to get my breath back," said Pippa when they came to a patch of grass and scrub on which a few juniper bushes grew.

She flopped down and Hal sat down beside her.

"Here, Fleck," he said, feeling in his pocket. "You can have your facecloth for a bit. I reckon you've earned it."

Fleck mouthed the facecloth and wagged a polite tail. But just then the dogs heard something interesting in the bushes and in a flash all five of them were off in pursuit.

"Was it a hare?" asked Hal.

Pippa shrugged. "I didn't see. But they must be very hungry. Maybe they'll catch something they can eat. They'll be back in a minute."

Pippa was right. The dogs returned presently. Whatever it was had been too fast for them. But when Hal patted Fleck he saw that Fleck had lost his facecloth.

"Where is it?" he asked his dog. "Where's your facecloth?"

Fleck looked down at the ground, then up at Hal, ran back a few paces and returned, while Hal looked at him, worried. Was there going to be a fuss? Up to now he had guarded his facecloth with his life.

But after a moment Fleck sat down and began contentedly to lick his paws. It didn't matter any longer where his facecloth was. When he bit Kevin, Fleck had tasted buttock blood, and a dog that has done that has moved a long, long way from facecloths.

19

Tracker Dogs

It was Curzon himself who took the call from Kevin on the hillside, and he hung up feeling extremely excited and pleased. What a breakthrough! The boy not only sighted but actually caught: imprisoned in a shed and only waiting to be picked up.

For a few moments Curzon, in his mind, spent the reward money that Donald Fenton would pay him. He wasn't so sure now about the yacht. A friend of his was building vacation homes on a Pacific island. Incredible houses they were, with five different swimming pools as well as the sea. Come to that, why wait till Fenton came up with the cash? Why not put down a deposit now? Leaning back in his chair, Curzon imagined himself standing on the top diving board, about to do a swallow dive into the turquoise water while a cluster of beautiful girls in bikinis watched him from below. Then he remembered that Sprocket had to be sent north at once to bring the boy back, and he picked up the phone again.

"Sprocket?" he barked. "I need you straightaway. You've got to go up north — the boy's been sighted."

"Yes, sir. I know. But I am up north already."

"Eh? What? What are you talking about?"

Curzon was completely confused. It was true he hadn't seen Sprocket all day, but he often didn't see him all day, and as a matter of fact he liked it better that way.

"I'm in Todcaster, sir," came Sprocket's patient voice. "I left you a message."

"Oh, you did, did you? I'm afraid the computer's down."

Actually what had happened was that Curzon had found what seemed to him a load of gobbledygook on his screen and simply erased it. He could never remember codes.

"Now listen carefully," he went on. "The message is

from someone called Kevin Dawks. He's on the road between Hilldale and Grant End." He read off Kevin's instructions. "'No policemen,' he said. He won't talk to anyone in uniform. Do you understand me?"

"Yes, sir. Absolutely. I'll make my way there at once."

Sprocket had had a miserable time in Todcaster. After driving through the night, he arrived at the circus to find the stable hand who had phoned him in a raging temper.

"He's split," he told Sprocket. "Must have pushed off last night, but it was him, all right, so I want some of that reward."

After that, Sprocket had questioned various people in the circus, who told him that the boy had gone back to his aunt Elsa, who had sent for him because her brother-in-law had to have an operation.

Anyone else might have given up then, but not Sprocket. Ferreting around, he learned that some children from a care home had come to the circus, and been seen talking to the boy. So he drove to Greystoke House and parked his van opposite the gates.

He had just got out his binoculars and was getting ready to do some serious investigating when a woman knocked on the window and asked him for a cauliflower.

"A nice firm one," she said, "but not too big. There's only the two of us now, with my daughter having gone off to London."

It was quite difficult to get rid of her, and in a way Sprocket blamed himself. If he had disguised the van as belonging to a plumber instead of a greengrocer, there would have been no bother. But though he had worked hard on his plumbing poem as he drove through the night, he hadn't been able to find a suitable rhyme for *toilet*. There was *oil it*, of course, but if there was one thing people didn't want near their lavatories, it was a lot of oil.

But there was worse to come. No sooner had he fixed his binoculars to his eyes than a fat woman burst through the gates and started threatening him.

"How dare you, you dirty old man!" she yelled. "I'll have the police after you, spying on innocent children."

As he drove away, Sprocket had been very upset. He was only twenty-six, and being called old was hurtful. So when his phone rang and he heard Curzon's message, his spirits soared. Stopping only to adjust his mustache and consult his road map (because the instruction book for the new sat nav seemed to be in Finnish) he set off for the village of Hilldale.

Kevin had come around to find his trousers torn, and both his backside and his nose still painful, but the knowledge that he would soon be a rich man consoled him. And the wretched boy had gone quiet at last; there was no sound from inside the shed.

His first sight of the white van coming up the track made him start to his feet angrily. He didn't want any bloomin' vegetables and what did the guy think he was doing, trespassing like that? But Sprocket's first words allayed his fears.

"Milton Sprocket, from MMM," he announced. "I gather you have the boy."

"I've got the boy, but have you got the money?"

"The money will be forthcoming," said Sprocket grandly. "As soon as I deliver the boy."

"All right," said Kevin. "Come on. He's in the shed there. I had a devil of a time keeping him in."

"Is he violent?" Sprocket asked anxiously. Children grew up very early these days, he knew, and they were strong. It was all that healthy food they were given to eat, and the exercise they took.

Kevin threw him a contemptuous glance. He unlocked the padlock, loosened the bolt, and stepped back.

Nothing happened.

"Come on out. I know you're in there."

Silence. Kevin made his way into the shed — and came out again.

"He's run off, the little . . ."

The language Kevin used surprised Sprocket. Some of the words he simply did not know, although he was a poet.

"He was in here," said Kevin when he had sworn himself to a standstill. "It was him, all right."

"I don't doubt it. He was seen in Todcaster last night."

"I won't be beaten by a squirt of a boy," said Kevin.

"But it's all right, I know a friend who'll help us find him. Come on. You can leave the van here."

"Where are we going?"

"We're going to see Colin. He'll put Darth and Terminator on the job. The boy won't get away from them, I promise you."

Darth and Terminator were dogs. Sprocket had to tell himself several times that that was what they were. They were not evil hounds, not monsters out of a hideous dream, but as the beasts growled and slavered and threw themselves against the wire fence of their enclosure it was hard to believe. When Kevin had explained that they were going to get hold of Colin's tracker dogs Sprocket had been nervous but excited. He hadn't taken the course on tracking with animals at his detecting college because it cost extra, but he knew all about bloodhounds, with their wrinkled faces and melancholy eyes, that could follow the scent of any human being.

But Darth and Terminator did not have wrinkled faces and they did not have melancholy eyes. They were grizzled, short-haired beasts, squat and barrel-chested with small ears and slightly bowed legs. And they were vicious. The pit bull in their ancestry was easy to see, but there were other strains there, and the whole animal, as Colin explained, was a high-powered machine for tracking anything in flight and running it to the ground.

As Colin let them out of their enclosure and snapped on their leashes, Sprocket allowed himself a question.

"They wouldn't harm the boy, would they? I don't think the reward will hold good if he's damaged at all."

"Nah, they're trained to a T," said Colin, spitting onto the grass. "They'll hold a runaway down but they wouldn't bite him. Unless I told them to tear him apart."

While the terrifying animals were loaded into the back of the pickup, Kevin put Sprocket in the picture. "There's no one knows more about tracking with dogs than Colin," he said.

It seemed that Colin had brought the sport of urban hunting to Todcaster. With Darth and

Terminator and a gang of friends with similar dogs, he went out at night after foxes that had come into town to raid the trash cans. Having no coverts to hide in, the foxes were easy prey.

"People wrote in and made a fuss," said Colin. "Didn't like their children finding headless foxes on the way to school." He laughed — a deep rumbling sound that shook his swollen belly. "Darth won't eat the back legs. He's a picky eater, is Darth."

They reached Kevin's lockup and the dogs bounded out. Sprocket gave Colin Hal's handkerchief and the dogs sniffed around the shed. Then suddenly they burst into excited cries and raced off up the hill.

"Told you," said Kevin. "He'll have taken to the moors."

The next hours were a nightmare for Sprocket, panting after Darth and Terminator as they strained at the ends of their leashes. The dogs kept up a steady pace and as they ran, there came from their throats an eerie, half-crazed baying — a sound to freeze the blood.

"You're sure they won't harm the boy?" Sprocket repeated from time to time, remembering the headless foxes.

"Gentle as lambs they'll be, when they've got him," said Colin.

And Sprocket could only say again that for a boy brought back in pieces in a garbage bag, nobody would pay a penny.

The hunt went on. They stumbled through bogs and over piles of last year's bracken. The weather was changing. A sharp wind had blown in from the sea, followed by the first spots of rain, and it was now that Sprocket felt a chill on his upper lip and realized that the worst had happened. Somewhere on the way he had lost his deeply loved mustache.

And still the terrifying beasts raced on.

Then, when Sprocket thought he could not go another step, the dogs checked, sniffed hard, circled . . . and suddenly took off in a different direction with a series of wildly excited yelps.

"They're getting close," shouted Colin over his shoulder. "I'm going to let them go."

He slipped off the leashes and the slavering beasts were off at speed, their noses down, sounding off in triumph.

"This is it! They've found him! There — behind those trees," shouted Colin. "Come on!"

He ran after the dogs and Kevin and Sprocket followed him. As they came into the copse, they saw that Colin was right. The hunt was over.

Darth and Terminator stood opposite each other, both tugging at something they held in their teeth, each dog claiming whatever it was as his own.

The men came closer and saw what it was. A blue facecloth.

It was not a good moment. The dogs showed no wish to go on with the hunt. As far as they could see they had done their job. They went on playing tug-of-war with their trophy while deep growls rumbled in their throats. Then when the facecloth came away in two halves, they settled down to devour their prizes.

"It's going to be a rough night," said Colin, turning up his collar against the rain. "We'd better get some shelter and try again in the morning. They'll pick up the scent again soon enough."

"What sort of shelter?" asked Sprocket nervously.

He was right to be nervous. Half an hour later they came to a shelter that Kevin knew about. It was nothing more than a rough, windowless hut with an earthen floor covered in sheep droppings. The wind roared through the cracks in the building. Water trickled down the walls.

Kevin and Colin did not seem to be bothered. They took out their hip flasks of whisky, belched, told a few stupid jokes, and were soon in a drunken sleep.

But for poor Sprocket, huddled in his jacket and as far away from the dogs as he could get, there was no sleep. He had never been so wretched in his life. He had put a few cookies into his pocket before he set off — the plain kind with no disturbing raisins or nuts that might scratch the lining of his stomach — but whenever he tried to put one in his mouth either Darth or Terminator came and fastened his teeth around his wrist till he had handed it over.

As the miserable hours passed and the rain beat down on the roof, Sprocket did his best to console himself. Perhaps if he brought the boy back safely, Curzon would allow him to come upstairs sometimes. Perhaps he would even let him have an office next to the beautiful Fiona. And perhaps, too, the awful writer's block that had attacked him would lift and he would be able to write his plumbing poem.

But it did not seem likely, and as the wretched night wore on there was worse to come. In a corner of the hut he heard the sound of one of the dogs being extremely sick. Shining his flashlight onto the ground, Sprocket saw — in a pool of vomit, the remnants of the blue facecloth, and beside it, covered in slime but still quite recognizable, his much-loved and sadly missed mustache.

Hal and Pippa, as they stumbled through the wildness of the night, would have been grateful even for a leaking, windowless hut in which to shelter. They were in the middle of the moor and hopelessly lost.

At first they had made good progress, navigating by the sun. Hal had even hoped that they might get to the coast that day. But very quickly the weather changed, the sun disappeared, and then came the darkness and the rain.

Both children had been brought up in town. The blackness of the night overwhelmed them. It was not just an absence of light, it was a malevolent force, and the rain did not come down only from the sky. It came from all sides, blown by the ceaseless wind. It ran down inside their hoodies; it drenched their shoes. And Hal was also suffering from delayed shock. The hour or so spent locked up in Kevin's shed had shaken him more than he realized at the time. He began to think that they would never reach the cottage by the sea — that they were doomed to fail.

"If we stop now, we'll probably die of exposure," said Pippa. "I never understood what that was, but I do now."

"We'll probably die of it whether we stop or not," muttered Hal.

They stumbled on, over boulders, across streams that were hardly wetter than the ground beneath their feet, and the faithful dogs followed. From Li-Chee, shorn of his pelt, came noises that were not very lion-like. He gave small snuffles of distress, and when Pippa picked him up he buried his nose in her jacket. The others padded on resolutely. Fleck was keeping up well; he seemed to have grown up since he had saved Hal from Kevin's clutches. And the dogs looked out for one another. If one of them for a moment vanished in the darkness, the others waited.

When they first saw a glimmer of light they hardly dared to believe it. They knew that people in the last stages of exhaustion see things that are not there. But the light was real. It grew stronger — and as they beat their way toward it they saw that it came from a tall, imposing building.

"It looks like a castle," said Pippa.

"Probably belongs to an ogre," murmured Hal. "Who else would live in the middle of nowhere?"

But whoever it belonged to, they had to go forward, and with the dogs pressing close behind them they made their way toward a great door. Even if whoever lived there was going to turn them in — even if he was going to eat them — they had no choice except to beg for shelter.

The bell clanged inside the great building and they waited. They were going to press it again when a slit opened in the door and a face appeared.

The face vanished and for a while nothing happened. Then slowly the door drew back and they saw a tall, hooded figure who stood there in silence.

"Please —" began Pippa. But she got no further because an awful thing now happened. Otto, the wise and gentle dog whom they would have trusted with their lives, had gone mad. A rumble came from his throat, and before they could stop him he reared up and with the full force of his weight, he landed with his paws on the shoulders of the hooded man.

The children started forward, horrified. This was the end of all their hopes of sanctuary. Then they saw what Otto was doing. He was licking the man's face. The rumble in his throat had become a kind of purring, and his tail went so fast that it had become a blur.

The hooded man allowed himself to be greeted like this for a few moments. Then gently he removed Otto's paws and came toward them.

"You are welcome, my children," he said.

"Can we bring the dogs in?" asked Pippa.

The tall man smiled.

"If you could not bring dogs into this place, it would be strange indeed."

20

Otto Remembers

They had come to the monastery of St. Roch. The tall man who had greeted them was the abbot, in charge of the monks who lived there, and now he led them along a corridor hung with paintings of various saints. It was warm and very quiet and there was a smell of beeswax and lilies. To the frozen children it seemed like paradise.

Otto did not follow the abbot. He walked beside him, his nose within inches of the abbot's robe.

"Of course," whispered Pippa. "Otto came from a monastery in Switzerland. The abbot there bred him himself, Kayley told me."

They were put in the charge of a round-faced monk with a friendly smile who introduced himself as Brother Malcolm and took them into a room where a fire burned brightly. Their wet clothes were peeled off and taken away and dry clothes brought in all sorts of shapes and sizes into which they fitted themselves as best they could. In a corner of the room, another monk was busy toweling the soaking dogs.

Then they were led into the refectory, where the monks were sitting at a long table, eating their supper. The abbot was in a carved seat at the top, while a very old monk, perched against a kind of high desk, was reading aloud from *The Lives of the Saints*.

The children slipped onto the end of a bench. Two bowls of soup were put before them, and two hunks of bread, and as they began to eat they saw that five bowls had been put down on the floor beside the wall, and the dogs, with their heads down, were eating hungrily.

After the soup came a dish of fruit. Hal managed to make out the shapes of the apples and pears; then they became blurred, and he could only just stop himself from falling forward with his head on his plate.

At the head of the table, the abbot made a sign, and Brother Malcolm came up to the children.

"You must be ready for your beds," he said.

He led Pippa and Hal out of the room, and Li-Chee, Francine, Honey, and Fleck followed close behind them. But not Otto. Otto gave an affectionate good-night lick to his friends, then padded over to the head of the table and flopped down with his great muzzle across the abbot's feet.

They followed Brother Malcolm up the stairs and along a silent corridor with a number of identical doors. They were hardly surprised anymore when he opened the first of the doors and they found a number of dog beds and a water bowl.

"It's like Goldilocks, only with dogs instead of bears," whispered Pippa, and Hal nodded.

There was no need to persuade Li-Chee and Francine and Honey to lie down. They had already chosen their beds and begun to turn themselves around and around, getting ready to settle down for the night. But Fleck stood beside Hal, waiting. He did not seem pathetic or frightened as he had done before when he expected to be separated from his master. It was rather that he felt that it was necessary to look after Hal, and Brother Malcolm picked this up at once.

"Perhaps he'd better stay with you tonight," he said.

Ten minutes later, Pippa was in bed in one of the small, whitewashed rooms that the monks kept for their guests, and Hal was in another, with Fleck on the floor beside him.

Hal fell asleep at once, but after an hour he was woken by a thump and found Fleck preparing to settle down on top of him.

"No, Fleck, get down," Hal ordered, looking at the spotless white cotton bedspread and remembering Albina's agitation about dogs on the coverlet. And as Fleck did not move: "You heard me. Dogs don't sleep on beds, it's not allowed."

Fleck got down, but reluctantly. The door was ajar, and he went out into the corridor, then back into the room, then out again.

"All right, if you want to go and sleep with your friends, I'll take you back there," said Hal, getting out of bed.

But as they passed the next door, which was ajar, Fleck stopped.

"What is it? What's the matter?"

Hal followed Fleck's gaze. Lying on the bed of what must have been a fairly portly monk were three retriever puppies. The monk was snoring gently, the bedspread going rhythmically up and down, and the dogs lying across him rose and fell also, soothed and lulled into the deepest of sleeps.

"OK, Fleck, you win," said Hal.

In less than five minutes Hal was asleep again, and his dog lay curled up at his side.

It was not until the following morning that Pippa understood about the place they had come to.

She had been too tired to take in anything much the night before, but now as she woke, she looked eagerly around her room. It was very plainly furnished, but there was one oil painting on the wall above her bed. It was of a man in sandals wearing a robe and carrying a staff. Around his head was a halo, and at his feet sat a dog holding a piece of bread in his mouth. It was a very nice dog, white with big black patches and concerned eyes. The bread was not for him, you could see that. It was for the man with the halo.

Underneath the picture, in gold letters, were the words *St. Roch*.

"Of course," said Pippa aloud. "I've been an idiot."

Her grandmother had been very devout and told her the stories of the saints. St. Roch had been a healer who looked after people with the plague until he caught the illness himself and went into the forest to die. But he didn't die because a dog brought him food from his master's table until he recovered. Saints usually have a bad time, being shot full of arrows or broken on wheels, but this dog, who did not even have a name, had saved him, and since then Roch had been the patron saint of dogs. He was the patron saint of other things, too — surgeons and people with knee problems and tile makers — but dogs were what he was famous for.

And this monastery was dedicated to his name!

Brother Malcolm, when he brought their dry clothes, told them more. "There is a picture of him in stained glass in our chapel window. As you will see, we try to carry on his work," he said.

The monks had already had their breakfast, but two places were laid for the children, with glasses of milk and home-baked bread and honey from the monk's own hives. And the dogs' breakfast, too, was waiting in their bowls.

But there was no sign of Otto, who had eaten earlier.

When they had finished their meal, Brother Malcolm took them through a door in the building and out into a walled garden. The weather had cleared; the air was soft and gentle after the storm. They walked between neatly kept herb beds and rows of young vegetables into an orchard full of blossoming apple trees. Under the trees stood a dozen beehives, which the dogs respectfully avoided.

"Is it true that you have to tell bees all the important things that happen?" asked Pippa. "Like when somebody dies."

Brother Malcolm turned to her. "Yes, it's true. Bees are messengers. They will carry anything you tell them straight up to God."

Hal had almost forgotten that they were on the run. He felt completely safe and contented. Perhaps he could be a monk when he grew up, he thought. It was true that monks couldn't get married, but from what he'd seen of married people that might be no bad thing.

The dogs had been snuffling about peacefully, but now they began to bark excitedly, while the whole of Li-Chee's back end quivered with pleasure. The children looked up to see the abbot coming toward them. Beside him, as though he had been there all his life, was Otto.

The abbot spoke quietly to Brother Malcolm, then turned to the children. "We've something to show you that you'll find interesting, I think," he said.

He led them to a low building standing by itself, and opened the door.

The floor of the room they entered was covered in a thick layer of straw and in the straw, playing and squealing and rolling over and over — was a host of puppies. The straw was golden in a shaft of sunlight and the puppies were golden, too. Retrievers with dark brown eyes and the softest of milk-filled stomachs.

"We breed guide dogs for the blind," said the portly monk who was in charge of them. "This litter is from a mother who comes from a long line of working dogs. We keep them till they're ready to go off for their training. Not all of them are suitable, but we've learned to pick out those who should go forward and the rest go to good homes."

He scooped up a very energetic puppy who was trying to make friends with Fleck.

"This one is very promising," he said. "Alert but not nervous."

The abbot nodded. "Brother Ambrose can tell when they're just a few weeks old."

"There's a guide dog who comes past the place where my sister works," said Pippa. "Grace, she's called. She's incredible."

The puppies were becoming overexcited, scurrying about all over the place as they tried to make friends with the visiting dogs. But now Otto took a few paces forward and sat down.

At once the puppies went to him and began to clamber over his legs, to play with his tail and dig their noses into his fur. Then carefully the huge dog rolled over onto his back, giving them even more places to climb, and with squeals of delight they crawled over his stomach, hung on to his ears. He had turned himself into a warm and living climbing frame and the abbot looked down at him with a glow in his eyes. It was almost as though Otto knew that each of these little creatures would one day be responsible for a person's safety and life.

But the time had come for the children to hear their fate and the abbot led them to a bench under the apple tree.

"Now," he said. "Tell me your story."

Hal turned anxiously to Pippa. She was usually the one who spoke for both of them, but though he was proud of Pippa's ability to make things up, he hated the idea of telling lies here in this place.

Pippa moved closer to the abbot and began to speak.

"It really started with Hal. His parents got him this dog and he thought it was for good, but after two days they took it back to Easy Pets and he was desperate and so was Fleck. I knew about it because my sister is the kennel maid there. . . ."

She went on to tell the abbot about her own brain-storm in letting the dogs go, their determination to reach Hal's grandfather in his cottage, what had happened in the circus and their mishaps with Kevin the Dumper. And Hal listened in amazement, for every word she spoke was true.

When she had finished, the abbot turned to Hal.

"Your grandfather's cottage is near here?"

Hal nodded. "It's down on the shore opposite Farra Island. He's a fisherman and he has a small farm there. If I could get to him before there's a fuss with my parents, he would understand."

"And you think he would take you in?" asked the abbot.

"Yes, I do. He's always thought I should have a dog."

"But five dogs? Has he always thought you should have five?"

Hal hung his head. It was true that all he and Pippa had thought of was getting safely to the cottage, but he could see how it would look to the abbot. Was it possible that they were going to be sent back or turned over to the police? They'd come so far, but even now a single phone call could end it all.

The abbot was silent, occasionally pulling one of Otto's ears. The minutes passed.

When he spoke, the words were solemn and slow.

"Since you're so near your journey's end I'll let you go on your way. But if I haven't had a telephone call within twenty-four hours to say that you have arrived safely, I shall straightaway call the police. Now go and find Brother Malcolm. He will give you some sandwiches and make sure you know the right path."

As they reached the building, the abbot went up the stairs with Otto, but the relief the children felt was mixed with anxiety. What of Otto, who had found his true place and his true master? Remembering Francine and Honey and what those two had suffered, they were very much afraid. Would Otto refuse to come? And what would it be like to finish the journey without him?

"It isn't for us to decide," said Hal. "The abbot will know."

When they were ready, the children and the other dogs waited at the front door. The abbot came downstairs with Otto at his side. He laid his hand on the great head.

"If God wills, we shall meet again," he said to him.

Otto made no fuss. He knew that his job was not yet done. He only moaned once, and pushed his muzzle against the abbot's robe. Then he turned and followed the children out of the door.

21

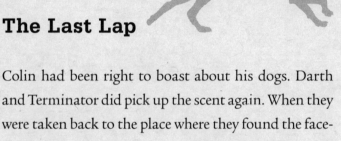

The Last Lap

Colin had been right to boast about his dogs. Darth and Terminator did pick up the scent again. When they were taken back to the place where they found the face-cloth, they circled for a while and then took off at speed, running out of the copse across the open moors.

Colin still held them on the leashes, and Kevin ran beside him, but poor Sprocket lagged badly behind. He was cold and hungry and tired, and his hand was wrapped in a handkerchief because Terminator had bitten him.

"Call that a bite?" Colin had jeered when Sprocket had cried out. "You wouldn't have a hand left if he'd bitten you. It's just a little nip, playful-like."

It had happened when Sprocket put his hand in his pocket to get out an indigestion pill, and Terminator thought he was reaching for a cookie that didn't seem to be coming his way.

I ought to get myself to a doctor and have an injection, thought Sprocket as he panted after the others. I could be in danger of getting tetanus, or even rabies.

And what was this mad runaway boy doing? He seemed to be heading toward the coast — but why? Was there a boat waiting to take him off? Was he part of an organized gang? The picture Curzon had shown him had been of a small, ordinary boy, but he seemed to be turning into a maniac.

The children left the monastery in high spirits. The sun was shining, larks sang, the heather was green and fresh after the rain. A well-made track led them gradually off the moor and down toward farmland. Hal knew that in a few hours he would be sitting in his grandfather's kitchen.

They passed a few isolated cottages and a farm, and then, at a place where the road curved around the hillside, they saw it at last — the sea! The North Sea can be gray and forbidding, but today it was like an ocean in a dream, blue-green and glittering with light, the white horses curling onto the golden sand. Hal had never visited his grandparents, but they had told him so much about where they lived, had drawn so many maps and pictures, that he felt as though he was coming home.

"Do you see that bay — the far one?" said Hal. "That's where the cottage is. Behind those dunes. I think we can take a shortcut across country."

They left the track and started to walk over rough pasture toward the coast.

But the dogs had become restless. They stopped with their noses in the air, sniffing and listening. And then the children heard what the dogs had already been aware of: the baying of hounds.

At first they took no notice. It was probably some kind of local hunt, people chasing after hares. Then they looked back and saw, rounding the bend on the road, three distinct figures. Two of them were in front, leading a couple of dogs. Now they stopped at the place where Hal and Pippa had left the track, while the dogs sniffed the ground, trying to pick up a scent.

Then suddenly one of the figures shouted and pointed while the other bent down and slipped off the leashes. The next moment, two dark, squat shapes leapt the low stone wall, and howling like creatures from the netherworld, they began to streak off down the hill.

Even then the children could not at first believe what they were seeing — it seemed impossible. Then suddenly they understood. It wasn't hares or foxes that these hounds were chasing.

"It's us they're after," shouted Pippa. "They're hunting us!"

Terrified, they began to race and slither down the steep slope and all the time the baying became louder. There was no moment when they dared to look behind them, so they did not notice that Otto was no longer there.

He had stopped at the edge of the last steep scramble down to the beach and was standing as still as if he were Barry, his stuffed ancestor in the Natural History Museum, his silhouette outlined against the high blue of the early summer sky.

The two hounds ran straight as arrows toward him, ignoring gorse, cowpats, a clump of barbed wire. The muscles in their chests and forelegs were bunched, their upper lips curled back, showing even more of their fearsome teeth. Their eyes were red, saliva streaked down their necks, and they had stopped barking. The shouting was over; the tearing and rending were about to begin.

Otto waited, perfectly still.

The pursuing beasts were only a few feet away from him now. With an immense effort they managed to stop themselves and adjusted their legs for the leap that would finish Otto and allow them to continue their headlong race for the boy. But for a moment they hesitated. The pit bull in them was ready for murder, but the bloodhound part wanted to get on with the chase.

And in this moment of indecision, Otto spoke. The growl started from somewhere in the lower abdomen and when it finally reached his voice box and emerged into the outside world it was like the sound of a mighty river swollen by rain as it thunders over great falls to the plain below.

At first nothing happened. The furious attacking dogs slavered and rumbled and grimaced. Then as Otto's endless growls rolled out over the grass, their attitude slowly changed. Their upper lips covered the ghastly fangs, their breathing quietened, their brows wrinkled in puzzlement. A small nervous yawn escaped each of them and slowly their gazes dropped to Otto's feet.

And then the two satanic beasts sank first their buttocks, and then — with their forepaws pushing gingerly forward — their bellies to the ground. They tried a last tremulous growl, but it had more than a touch of squeak in it.

As if to say, "No. Not a single word more," Otto finally lowered his head, took a step forward, and opened his mouth. And at the other end of these two terrors of the night, something odd occurred. A small tremor seemed to affect their stumpy tails. Could it be a nervous twitch? But no. It came again, and it was getting stronger . . . and stronger still.

For the first time since they were puppies playing happily at their mother's side, Darth and Terminator were wagging their tails.

And down on the beach, Hal and Pippa and the other dogs raced along the sands, burst through the doors of the cottage, and tumbled in a heap into the hall.

22

The Sea, the Sea!

Hal's grandmother was crying. She wasn't pretending not to as she bustled around making tea, buttering bread, and opening cookie tins. Throughout the ghastly week in which they had waited for news of Hal, Marnie had been brave and hopeful for her husband's sake, but now she let go.

The kitchen of the cottage seethed with dogs and children. Otto had padded in quietly when his job was done, and Meg the old Labrador had come out from under the sofa and was doing her best to be polite to the newcomers.

In the middle of the throng sat Fleck, looking very pleased with himself. Hal's grandfather had greeted him by name as soon as he had stopped hugging Hal.

"Hello, Fleck," he had said, picking him out as the dog who mattered, whose place this was. "Welcome to our home." Already, Fleck had taken charge of one of Marnie's slippers and was keeping it safe.

Hal, perched on a stool by the kitchen table, was completely happy. It was all as he had hoped. His grandparents, so warm and understanding, the crackling fire, the view outside the window of the sea and the islands and the scudding clouds . . . Only it was even better than he had imagined because he had saved not only Fleck but the other dogs, and he had found Pippa!

But when the children began to speak of their adventures, the horror of the last hour came back in full force.

"We were chased by tracker dogs," said Pippa. "Honestly. We couldn't believe at first that it was us they were after."

"It was as though we were criminals," said Hal. "You never saw such animals. If it hadn't been for Otto —"

He broke off, because the back door of the cottage had opened and in the threshold stood a large, uniformed policeman, looking very much at home.

"Afternoon," he said, removing his cap.

The children froze. Had they been betrayed? Were they going to be packed off to London and the dogs imprisoned again? Was it possible that Hal's grandparents were going to turn them in? For a moment, Hal's whole world seemed to topple.

But the policeman had begun to speak.

"I just called in to see if you'd had any news of the boy," he said, "but I see that all's well."

"Yes, thanks, Arthur. Hal's safe and sound and so is his friend Pippa. It was what we thought. He came with Fleck here. But the children have just told us they were chased by tracker dogs. Can you believe it?"

The policeman nodded. "We've had a message from one of the farmers out on the moor. I've sent a couple of men up there now. We reckon we know who they are. Chap called Kevin Dawks and his friend. Kevin's a dumper and they're nasty pieces of work, both of them. They're breaking the law, of course, tracking without a license."

He put his cap on again, shook hands with the children, and left.

"He's been such a comfort," said Marnie. "Came in every day to see if you'd turned up. The police never thought you'd been kidnapped. They always thought you were on the way to us."

But now it was time for the telephone. The call to the abbot didn't take long, but Pippa's call home was not quite so simple. It was Kayley who answered the phone.

"We've been expecting you back from camp for an hour. Is the bus late?"

"Actually, I'm not at camp," said Pippa. "I'm in Northumberland."

"You are *what*?"

"I'll explain. Only it's a long story."

There was a pause. Then, "Is it a story about dogs?" asked Kayley.

"Yes, it is." Pippa took a deep breath. "That's exactly what it is. I've got them here with me and . . ." She launched into an explanation.

When she hung up, she looked distinctly shaken.

"My sister's coming to fetch me," she said. "I hope that's all right. She's a bit cross."

Actually, considering how good-tempered Kayley usually was, she had not been a bit cross. She had been very cross indeed.

"Now you, Hal," said his grandfather.

In London, Albina picked up the phone and shrieked.

"Oh, thank goodness! Thank the Lord! Oh, Hal, we've been so worried, I thought I would die! You must come back at once — at once. Is there an airplane you can get? Or perhaps the train's faster. No, what am I saying? Of course we'll come up and fetch you in the car. We'll be with you in a few hours."

Hal's voice cut in, quiet but implacable.

"I'm not coming home," he said.

"What? Oh, Hal, darling, what are you saying? Hal . . ." She began to sob down the telephone but her son did not relent. He was reliving the moment when he had come back from the dentist and found Fleck gone.

"I'm here with Fleck and I'm not going to give him up. Not ever."

"No, no . . . of course not. I'm sorry. It'll be all right, we understand."

"You tricked me," said Hal. "I don't trust you anymore." Albina was still crying, but Hal was seeing Fleck lying unconscious on the floor of his cage. "I'll never trust you again."

He was about to put down the receiver when his grandfather came and took it out of his hand.

"Albina, I'd like to speak to my son, please," he said. "Is he there?"

"Yes, he's here. Oh, what shall I do?" Albina was beside herself. "Donald, it's your father."

Donald took the phone.

"You've got the boy?"

"Yes, he's safe and sound and he's got his dog. But he's very tired and at the end of his rope. Give him a few days to rest up before you come."

"But that's ridiculous. You can't expect us not to —"

His father's voice was different. Not the voice of someone who had decided to stand aside and not interfere. This was his father's voice as he remembered it from his childhood.

"The boy needs time. Come up at the end of the week. And remember this, Donald: If you try to take his dog away, you'll have lost him for good."

Returning to the kitchen, Alec found his wife and the children with their faces pressed to the window.

"We saw them," said Pippa gleefully. "In a police van. The dumper was there and another man and two dogs. And there was someone else with them, sort of cowering at the back. He looked terrified."

She spoke the truth. Milton Sprocket, arrested by the police, hemmed in by Darth and Terminator, cold and bitten and disgraced, had sunk to the very depths of his being.

23

Return of the Dogs

On the following day Hal was out in the garden helping his grandfather weed the vegetable bed when he saw an enormous silver car drive up to the cottage.

Immediately he was furious. His parents had promised not to come up before the end of the week. What's more, they had bought another car they didn't need — a Rolls-Royce gleaming with newness.

The car stopped, and out of the driver's seat came a calm-faced Indian gentleman who stood for a moment looking at the view. Then a second door opened, and out stepped Kayley.

•   •   •

When she had finished talking to Pippa on the telephone, Kayley had hurried around to find her mother, who was sewing with Mrs. Naryan. It was no good trying to shield Pippa now, so she explained exactly what had happened.

"I'm going up to fetch her straightaway," she said. "Goodness knows what else she'll get up to. There's an overnight bus to Berwick, I can catch that. I've got enough in my savings for the fare, just about."

But at this point Mrs. Naryan put down her needle.

"That is not a good idea, I think," she said in her soft voice. "This bus will not be pleasant."

She walked out of the room and came back with her husband. Mr. Naryan, like his wife, was small, soft-spoken, and gentle. He was also one of the richest men in England, having built up a flourishing import-export business in the years since he had left Rajasthan.

"I will drive you to Northumberland," he said.

And when both Kayley and her mother said no, no, it was out of the question, it was impossible, he only smiled. "There is a man in the north whom I would like to see," he said. "I will come to your house at six tomorrow morning."

Now he shook hands with Hal's grandparents and then took his leave. He was going to spend the night in a hotel farther up the coast and come back for Kayley and Pippa on the following day.

The dogs remembered Kayley. They remembered her so well that she was nearly knocked over, and Kayley petted them and talked to them as only she could talk to dogs.

But her greeting to her sister was not so enthusiastic.

"Come outside," she said to Pippa when she had been welcomed by Hal's grandparents and said hello to Hal.

The first ten minutes as they walked along the beach was spent by Kayley giving Pippa a piece of her mind.

"You must have been crazy," she said. "We've had the police around, and the Carkers are spitting blood. I thought you'd forgotten to set off the burglar alarm, but letting the dogs out on purpose . . ."

"I know," said Pippa. "I sort of saw red. The way they looked when Hal took Fleck away . . . I couldn't bear it."

"That's all very well, but what now? Hal's grand-parents can't keep five dogs. What's going to become of them? If we take them back to Easy Pets, it'll come out that you let them go, and —"

"We can't," Pippa broke in. "We absolutely can't take them back to sit in those awful cages again."

"Well, how can we find homes for them?"

Pippa looked at the four dogs who had followed them onto the sands.

"They've got homes, Kayley. All four of them. They found homes for themselves, but they came on with us to see Fleck safe. They've found homes and work and masters that they want to serve."

"What do you mean?" asked Kayley.

So Pippa told her.

•   •   •

They left early the following day. Mr. Naryan was a Buddhist and didn't seem to mind dogs piling into his beautiful car. The Buddha held all life to be sacred, and whether it was a businessman or a Saint Bernard lolling on his spotless cream upholstery made no difference to him.

Fleck said good-bye again and again to Otto and Honey and Francine and Li-Chee, and they said it to him. But the little mongrel was not worried or upset. He had known at once that he and Hal belonged to the cottage in a special way, and when the others got into the car, he turned and went back into the house and flopped down contentedly beside old Meg.

For Hal it was more difficult. He and Pippa hadn't been together long, but those days on the road had changed him. He'd be able to write to Pippa and phone her, but seeing the dogs go was hard.

It was Kayley who comforted him.

"You'll see them again, Hal," she said. "When you've shared so much with someone, whether it's a dog or a person, they don't just go out of your life."

• • •

They drove to the monastery first. As the car slowed down, Otto, who had been looking out of the window, began to moan and gargle deep in his throat, and to press his nose against the glass. They stopped outside the gates to let him out, and Pippa and Kayley went with him. Pippa was putting up her hand to ring the bell, but before she could do so the door opened and Brother Malcolm stood there, smiling his welcome.

But now it all went wrong. She had expected Otto to rush inside and up the stairs, but he wouldn't go. Instead he turned and raced away around the side of the building and out of sight.

"He is in the garden," said Brother Malcolm.

"We'd better go and see," said Kayley.

The girls walked past the herb beds and into the orchard, where they saw an unusual sight. The abbot of St. Roch lay on the grass, felled like an oak tree. And over him and beside him and around him was Otto, now licking, now barking, now simply sitting on his chest.

"Is it all right?" shouted Pippa.

The abbot did not reply. He merely raised one arm — perhaps in blessing, perhaps in greeting, perhaps just because it was the only one of his limbs that he could free.

The girls did not repeat their question. If ever anything was all right, this was. They turned and walked back to the car.

Old Selby, the shepherd, was getting ready to load his possessions into the moving van. There weren't many of them. His room in Rosewood was small, and everything was built in and fitted. He'd set the bonfire, ready to burn the stuff he wasn't taking, and now he picked up his crook and laid it across the top. Billy was going to a farmer in the neighboring valley. He padded miserably behind his master, his eyes clouded with anxiety, and from time to time he lifted his head and howled.

All the same, it was Billy who first heard the car purring down the track. His ears went up. He yapped once as the door opened.

"Go, Honey," said Pippa. "It's all right. You can go now."

Honey bounded out, came back once to her friends, and then was gone.

But Pippa, following her, stopped in dismay, seeing the moving van, the bonfire.

"Oh dear," she said. "You're leaving! We'd hoped you'd be able to have Honey, but if —"

Old Selby was bending down, gently rubbing Honey's head.

Now he straightened himself. "No, I'm not," he said. "I'm not leaving now. I'm staying right here where I belong."

He walked over to the bonfire and picked out his stick. Then he went over to the driver of the van.

"I've changed my mind," said Selby. "You'll have to take the van back."

The driver looked at him, ready to argue. Old people had fancies, he knew. The shepherd probably didn't know what he was doing.

But then he looked at Selby again. When he first saw him, he'd taken him for a man near the end of his life, but he seemed to have changed. He didn't really look old at all — and the driver shrugged and got back into his cab.

"Come on, Honey," said Selby. "We've got work to do."

• • •

They caught the circus in Todcaster on its last day. The big top had come down; trucks were being loaded. Francine was out of the car, streaking away the moment it stopped. Kayley and Pippa, following her, heard her yapping outside one of the caravans. Then a black shape bounded out, and in a moment, Rupert and Francine were dancing around each other in a frenzy of joy.

Now a thin man in a beret followed Rupert out of the trailer and introduced himself as Petroc.

"This must be the dog that George told me about. Francine, is it?" he asked in a slight foreign accent.

"Yes, it is. We wondered if she could stay with you?"

Petroc sighed. "It would have been good. She could have joined my act, Petroc's Poodles. It is the best dog act in the world," he said modestly. "But a dog like that is worth a lot of money and I am a poor man, so I'm afraid —"

"We don't want any money," said Kayley quickly. "We just want her to be happy."

Petroc looked at Francine, rolling over and over

with Rupert on the grass. His thin face creased into a smile.

"She is happy, I think," he said. "Yes, I know dogs and this one is happy. She is very happy indeed."

But Francine did not forget her manners. She gave a paw to Kayley, then to Pippa, then to Kayley once again, before she followed Rupert into the trailer and her new life.

The car was empty now and Li-Chee was getting worried. He had whimpered pathetically when Otto left, and now he sat on Pippa's knee, his pop eyes anxiously searching her face. Where was everybody? Had he been forgotten?

Kayley and Pippa, too, were nervous. This last stop was going to be difficult. What if there was a rule against having pets in the care home? Mr. Naryan, driving steadily, said little, but he was a comfort.

"He has a big heart, that one," he said. "It will be well with him."

As they turned into the drive of Greystoke House, they saw that the garden was full of children. They stopped and Li-Chee jumped out — and then from the group of children one little girl came running like the wind.

"Li-Chee," said Nini, and now she did not kneel to him but scooped him up in her arms.

Then Mick came over and Pippa gave him the note that Hal had written.

"We made it all right, thanks to you, and your friends," she said, and Mick said it was nothing, and that Nini had been quite different since the night they came.

"She talks now and she sort of fits in. It's great."

But the difficult part was still to come. Mick took them to Mrs. Platt's office, but they had to be careful because the housemother knew nothing about the night in the boiler room.

Pippa said they were looking for a home for the Peke.

"We remembered that Nini liked him so much when she came to the circus. But perhaps there's a rule against having animals here?"

Mrs. Platt said no, there wasn't. In fact, at the last meeting of the committee it had been suggested that the children might have a dog. "There was a very nasty character in a white van out there the other day," she said. "Sat there for hours. I thought then a dog might see him off." She went to the window. "My goodness, that's not much of a watchdog, though. It looks like a little rat. Is that the one in the circus act? What's happened to his hair?"

Kayley looked at Pippa, who was the family liar.

"A horrible boy cut it because he was jealous," said Pippa. "Our dog act was better than his."

Mrs. Platt was shocked. "People don't know how to discipline children these days." She looked out of the window again. "But really, I don't think —"

She broke off. Li-Chee, who had been sitting on Nini's lap, suddenly raced down the steps, barking at the top of his voice.

"It's the newspaper delivery boy," said Mrs. Platt. "Well, I reckon I was wrong about him not being a watchdog."

"Pekes are amazing like that," said Kayley. "They're lion dogs, bred to protect emperors and give notice of danger."

"Are they, then?" said Mrs. Platt, looking at the newspaper boy who had dropped the paper and run back to the gate. "Well, well — I guess he can stay."

The last thing Kayley and Pippa saw as they drove away was Li-Chee sitting on the top of the steps. Nini was on one side of him and Mick on the other, but Li-Chee's paws were stretched out in front of him and he held his head high.

Just so had his ancestors sat and guarded the palaces of emperors. And just so sat Li-Chee now, protecting Greystoke House.

24

Albina Grovels

Albina was on the floor on her hands and knees, making odd noises, clucking noises, then cooing noises, then wheedling noises. The floor was not the carpeted floor of her London house, it was the rough-boarded floor of the cottage, covered only in a worn rug.

"Please, Fleck, please. I'm sorry," she said. "I didn't mean it. Please come out and let's be friends."

Hal's parents had arrived an hour earlier. Hal had allowed himself to be embraced, but only politely. And Fleck had taken one look at Albina, growled horribly, and vanished under the sofa.

"It's no good," said Hal. "He'll never forget what you did."

"Can't you make him come out?" begged Albina.

"No. And if I could, I wouldn't," said Hal.

Donald had gone out with his parents to look at the boat, and Hal and his mother were alone.

Albina tried again. Marnie had given her a bone and she waggled it back and forward under the sofa, but Fleck ignored it. Groveling on the floor, she went on making what she hoped were wooing noises. Then she put her hand under the sofa and pulled it back with a cry as Fleck's teeth fastened on her fingers.

"Oh, what shall I do?" she cried, getting to her feet. "Look at my tights, they're ruined. And my skirt." She went over to the table and sat down. Then she let her head fall forward onto her hands and began to sob.

For a few moments Hal, sitting opposite, just let her cry. Then something horrible happened. The anger he had felt with his parents began to get weaker . . . and weaker still. He missed it badly, this rage that had kept him going on his adventure. But there was nothing to be done about it; it was gone.

His mother had done a wicked thing; she was foolish and misguided — but she was his mother.

He put an arm around Albina.

"It's all right," he said. "It's over. It's all right."

And at that moment Fleck came out from under the sofa and trotted over to the table. It was "forgiving time," it seemed, and he flopped down between Albina and Hal, and yawned, and went to sleep.

Later that afternoon, Hal went for a walk along the dunes with his father. The last week, when he'd not known whether his son was dead or alive, had changed Donald Fenton. It was as though Hal's love for his grandparents made him see his old home as he had seen it when he was a boy. He no longer felt like sneering at the shabby cottage, the old boat with its temperamental engine. While Hal was with his mother, Donald had been out and emptied the lobster pots, and helped Alec fix the pump on the *Peggotty*. It was a screwdriver that Donald now wore behind his ear, not a gadget connecting him with New York.

"You really like it up here, don't you?" said Donald.

"Yes, I really do. And so does Fleck."

Donald sighed. Fleck was here to stay, but he was not going to make life easier.

"What about Okelands? We took a lot of trouble getting you in there."

"I'm not going to boarding school," said Hal. "I told you, I'm not leaving Fleck. What I'd like to do is stay here and live with my grandparents. There's a school in Seaville."

"Yes, I know. I was there for seven years."

Hal looked up at his father. He was staring out at the sea and he looked stern — or was it sad?

"You like it so much better here than being with us? Than being at home?" asked Donald, and Hal could not help hearing the hurt in his voice.

"It's not exactly like that," said Hal. "I wouldn't like never to be at home again." He thought of the blond girl in the park, and Joel, the school friend he'd been pretending to stay with, and now of course there was Pippa. And his parents, who had got everything so wrong but who were trying now. Perhaps in their own way they had always tried.

"Could I stay here for another month? I've missed so much school anyway. Then I'll get Fleck trained."

Donald turned to his son and smiled with relief. There wasn't going to be a battle. Hal was going to come home.

"I don't see why not," he said. "I'll come and fetch you, and spend a few days. It's time I had a break."

But people do not change completely, however hard they try.

"I'd like to buy you something really nice, Hal. It can cost as much as you like. I mean it — the sky's the limit."

Hal looked at him for a long time.

"All I ever wanted was a dog," he said.

But as Donald's face fell, Hal had an idea. "Actually, there is something I'd like. I'd like it a lot, but it's not exactly for me. It's for Pippa's family. I'd never have made it here if it wasn't for Pippa. They're really hard up. If you could help them, then perhaps they could start up something for themselves. Kayley shouldn't be working for Mr. Carker anyway. He's an awful man. Maybe they wouldn't have to know where the money came from?"

Donald nodded.

"Consider it done," he said, and they turned and made their way back to the cottage.

25

What Happened to the Carkers

Kayley sat in her little office at Easy Pets. She had been working since seven in the morning, making a register, alone and without pay in the deserted building, and she was absolutely exhausted.

Just a week after she brought Pippa back from Northumberland, Kayley had come to work as usual and found that the Carkers had disappeared. They had put in such a ridiculous insurance claim for the missing dogs that the accountants had started to look into their affairs, and it was found that they had been cheating on their income tax for years and years.

So the charming couple had fled to Spain, owing Kayley her wages and leaving only enough food for a couple of days for the dogs.

Fortunately, a charity that cared for animals in distress had stepped in to try and find homes for the abandoned dogs. Because the Easy Pets dogs were highly bred and had been well looked after, plenty of people had come forward to offer to have them, but Kayley had absolutely insisted on inspecting every single home to make sure that it was suitable for the dogs she had cared for and knew so well. Now she only had to check the list of new owners and the job was done.

Well, almost done. All the dogs were happily housed, except for one. No one had come forward offering to have Queen Tilly. She sat now on her hot water bottle, shrieking and twitching and shaking with ill temper, the only dog left in the huge building that only a week ago had been full of life.

"Oh, what on earth shall I do with you?" Kayley asked her.

She would have taken her home herself if it hadn't

been for her landlord, who forbade all pets. Kayley had pity even for this most unattractive dog.

It was as she was standing by Queen Tilly's cage that the doorbell rang.

Outside on the steps stood a rather forlorn-looking young man.

"The name is Sprocket," he said.

A lot had happened to Milton Sprocket since he had followed Darth and Terminator across the moors and been picked up in a police van.

The disgrace, for a detective, of falling into the hands of the force was overwhelming, but even worse was the terror he had felt at being cooped up with the two tracker dogs, slavering and frothing and showing their teeth only a few inches away from him. Darth and Terminator wanted to make it clear that though Otto had stopped them in their tracks, they were still killing machines, and whenever Sprocket tried to move his cramped limbs, their lips curled back over their incisors and they growled like the hounds of the underworld.

Though Sprocket had been released almost

straightaway and been able to get back to his van and drive to London, he had been left with a serious trauma. It was a kind of mental illness: a terror not just of dangerous dogs but of all dogs. Even a dog walking along on the other side of the road brought on an attack, causing him to shake all over.

This was obviously very inconvenient for a detective. A man with a false mustache shaking like a leaf was apt to attract attention. Nothing could be done about the tragic block over his poetry, thought Sprocket, but surely he could find somebody who would help him to overcome his fear of dogs? So he had consulted a doctor, who had sent him to another doctor, who told him that the only way to be cured was to have a dog of his own.

Sprocket had never been a dog lover. There was too much chewing and slobbering involved for a neat and careful man like himself. On the other hand, his work was suffering. Then he had a brain wave. He would rent a dog from an agency, just for an hour or two. If it brought on an attack, he could always bring it straight back. Perhaps he could start with half an hour, then an hour. And the dogs could gradually get bigger. It would be expensive, but he was no longer so hard up. His aunt had died and left him some money and he hoped one day to set up on his own.

And thinking about dog hire agencies, he remembered passing one on the way north, and drove to Easy Pets.

The girl who let him in was pretty and gentle and nice. Sprocket took to her at once, but she had sad news to give him.

"I'm afraid we're closed down. The owners have left, and we've had to find homes for the dogs. I wish we could help you but you see . . ." She waved her arm at the empty cages, the bare floors, the garbage bags waiting to be collected.

"Oh dear. Well, I'll just have to try somewhere else."

He was turning to go when a high-pitched and angry yapping broke the silence.

"She's the last dog left," said Kayley. "We can't find a home for her, I'm afraid. I don't know what will happen. . . ."

She led Sprocket into Room A where the Mexican

hairless in her cage was screaming and twitching and shivering with loneliness and rage.

"Goodness." Sprocket had never seen such an unappealing dog.

"I'm afraid she gets the gripes from time to time," said Kayley.

Sprocket stared at her and his mouth dropped open because an absolutely amazing thing had happened. The dreadful block that had stopped him from writing poetry had disappeared. It was the word *gripes* that did it. For what was *gripes* except the perfect rhyme for *pipes*. And, as if it had been lowered down from heaven, the completed couplet came to him.

If your toilet's got the gripes,

We will come and fix your pipes.

It was pithy, it was exact, and there was nothing in it that his mother would think was rude.

In her cage, Queen Tilly was still twitching and shivering and screaming and Sprocket, looking at her, wondered what she reminded him of. Then suddenly it came to him. Of course. Himself. He had been like that all through his school days, shivering and twitching and wanting to scream. Unwanted. Unloved.

He took a deep breath. He couldn't do it. It was impossible.

But in his mind he had already done it. After all, this revolting little creature had given him back his gift for poetry. Perhaps she would turn out to be his lucky charm.

The relief of having found a home for Queen Tilly kept Kayley going on the long journey on the train, but when she got home she flopped down on the sofa, thoroughly miserable. She'd lost her job and the dogs who had been her friends, and the loss of her wages would make things really hard for the family.

"It's all right, love," said her mother. "I've got my sewing with Mrs. Naryan, and you'll find something else to do. A girl like you won't be out of work for long."

But jobs were hard to get, and Kayley didn't have a lot of paper qualifications. When she'd phoned about a vacancy in a boarding kennel they'd asked her if she had a Diploma in Domestic Canine Management. Without it, the lady thought, she would find it hard to muck out the dogs' cages or take them for a walk!

Pippa came in then from school, followed by the twins, and everybody did their best to cheer Kayley up, but what had happened at Easy Pets had shaken them all.

They were sitting down to their supper when a black car drew up outside the window. An expensive-looking car, out of which stepped a smartly dressed man with a briefcase.

"What does he want, I wonder," said Mrs. O'Brian, looking worried. "We've paid our rent."

"They'll be inspecting something," said Pippa gloomily.

The doorbell rang.

"I'd like to speak to Miss Kayley O'Brian, please," said the man with the briefcase. "Is this the right house?"

"Yes," said Pippa, who had opened the door. "I suppose you'd better come in."

Albina was shopping. It was her favorite occupation and she was entirely happy. The three G aunts were with her. Hal was coming home in a week's time and she was getting ready.

The shop was called the Pampered Pooch and it sold everything that a well-turned-out dog might need. A famous dress designer had just produced a new range of tartan jackets and matching booties for afternoon wear, and for more athletic dogs there were jumpsuits of mink or ermine. Displays of jeweled collars were arranged on satin cushions. There were diamond studs for dogs to wear in their ears, and gold ribbons to plait into their mustaches, and inflatable ham bones that played "Silent Night" for dogs that found it difficult to sleep. Kennels shaped like paddle steamers or railway stations or giant boots stood on the floor, there was a stand of motoring goggles for dogs with sensitive eyes, and the shelves groaned with bubble baths and scents and deodorants for dogs that worried about their personal hygiene.

"Oh dear, I don't know where to begin," said Albina. "There's so much. Do you think Fleck would like a pillow shaped like a frankfurter sausage?"

Geraldine had found a cashmere bonnet for cold days with a ribbon to tie under the chin, and Gloria had fallen for a blanket that played "Hush-a-bye, Poochie" when you picked it up.

The ladies ran hither and thither, getting more and more excited.

"Look, here's a collar with real garnets," said Glenda. "I think garnets would suit him, don't you? And it would go with your bracelet, wouldn't it?"

Albina took it from her hand.

"Yes, it would. Though there's an even better one over there. Look! It's in alligator skin with a double row of rhinestones and the clasp is sixteen-carat gold."

They picked up a bottle of scent called Doggie Delirium and put it to their noses.

"It's heavenly. He must have some of that," said Gloria.

She looked at the price and gave a little shriek, but really the expense didn't matter. Spending a lot of money was what it was all about.

"There's some canine mascara here," said Glenda. "I seem to remember his eyelashes were rather pale."

They were piling up their purchases, ready to take them to the counter, when they saw an object that stopped them in their tracks. For a moment they could not even speak, it was so beautiful and wonderful and strange. A platinum pooper scooper set with opals and amethysts.

Albina reached for it with a shaking hand.

"It's copied from a design that was used by the Russian royal family," she said, reading the label. "Oh, I must have that, I absolutely must!"

But just as she was about to add it to the other objects they had chosen, something happened. Albina straightened herself. She stood stock-still and a kind of judder went through her. A sort of twitch . . . And then slowly, very slowly (because it was so diffi-cult) she put back the bottle of Doggie Delirium, and the blanket that played "Hush-a-bye, Poochie," and the rhinestone collar, and last of all, with a stab of real pain, the pooper scooper made of platinum.

"No," said Albina, being nobler than she had ever been in her life. "I've decided. I'm not going to buy anything till Hal comes home. I'm going to wait. It is for Hal to choose."

And with the G aunts following, she marched out of the shop.

•   •   •

Hal was reading a letter. He sat on an overturned boat on the shore. The sun was shining and the North Sea was on its best behavior, silver near the shore, shading to pale blue and then a deep azure. The tide was out and the sands stretched for miles, empty and golden, as they do on the Northumbrian coast.

Fleck sat at his feet, but the letter was a long one.

"All right, Fleck, you can go and explore," said Hal — and Fleck looked up at him and then trotted off along the beach.

The letter was from Pippa, and as he read it, Hal smiled, for his father had done exactly what Hal had asked of him. And done it secretly.

. . . It's absolutely extraordinary because it happened just when Kayley came home after she finished at Easy Pets and she was feeling really rotten. Apparently one of the people who used to rent dogs noticed how good Kayley was with animals and he put her name down for a grant from a charity that looks after animals. It's a huge sum and of course it's all tied up with endowments and things. I don't really understand the details, but it means that Kayley can do what she's always wanted to do: start an animal rescue place where the

animals are cared for properly and never have to be put down even if they're sick and can't find homes. We've looked at a patch of land not too far away and there's a little house — it's not much more than a hut at the minute, but we're all going to pitch in and make it habitable. Isn't it fantastic? You'll come and help, won't you? And maybe that nice maid Olga you told us about? We're going to call it Fillongley after the family farm. Grandfather's over the moon. . . .

Hal looked up. He'd go and phone his father and thank him.

But where was Fleck? There was no sign of him on the long, deserted beach. For a moment, Hal was overcome by panic. Had he got lost, or drowned, or stolen? It wasn't like him to go so far on his own.

He put his fingers in his mouth and whistled — and a white speck appeared, grew larger, and flopped down at Hal's feet. Fleck's tongue lolled, his tail thumped on the sand. He seemed to be smiling. . . .

A dog who belongs to somebody forever is a dog who is free.